Macbeth

William Shakespeare

The Tragedie of Macbeth

Actus Primus. Scoena Prima.

Thunder and Lightning. Enter three Witches.

  1. When shall we three meet againe?
In Thunder, Lightning, or in Raine?
  2. When the Hurley-burley's done,
When the Battaile's lost, and wonne

3. That will be ere the set of Sunne

     1. Where the place? 2. Vpon the Heath

3. There to meet with Macbeth

1. I come, Gray-Malkin

  All. Padock calls anon: faire is foule, and foule is faire,
Houer through the fogge and filthie ayre.

Exeunt.

Scena Secunda.

Alarum within. Enter King, Malcome, Donalbaine, Lenox, with
attendants, meeting a bleeding Captaine.

  King. What bloody man is that? he can report,
As seemeth by his plight, of the Reuolt
The newest state

  Mal. This is the Serieant,
Who like a good and hardie Souldier fought
'Gainst my Captiuitie: Haile braue friend;
Say to the King, the knowledge of the Broyle,
As thou didst leaue it

Cap. Doubtfull it stood,
As two spent Swimmers, that doe cling together,
And choake their Art: The mercilesse Macdonwald
(Worthie to be a Rebell, for to that
The multiplying Villanies of Nature
Doe swarme vpon him) from the Westerne Isles
Of Kernes and Gallowgrosses is supply'd,
And Fortune on his damned Quarry smiling,
Shew'd like a Rebells Whore: but all's too weake:
For braue Macbeth (well hee deserues that Name)
Disdayning Fortune, with his brandisht Steele,
Which smoak'd with bloody execution
(Like Valours Minion) caru'd out his passage,
Till hee fac'd the Slaue:
Which neu'r shooke hands, nor bad farwell to him,
Till he vnseam'd him from the Naue toth' Chops,
And fix'd his Head vpon our Battlements

King. O valiant Cousin, worthy Gentleman

Cap. As whence the Sunne 'gins his reflection,
Shipwracking Stormes, and direfull Thunders:
So from that Spring, whence comfort seem'd to come,
Discomfort swells: Marke King of Scotland, marke,
No sooner Iustice had, with Valour arm'd,
Compell'd these skipping Kernes to trust their heeles,
But the Norweyan Lord, surueying vantage,
With furbusht Armes, and new supplyes of men,
Began a fresh assault

King. Dismay'd not this our Captaines, Macbeth and
Banquoh?
Cap. Yes, as Sparrowes, Eagles;
Or the Hare, the Lyon:
If I say sooth, I must report they were
As Cannons ouer-charg'd with double Cracks,
So they doubly redoubled stroakes vpon the Foe:
Except they meant to bathe in reeking Wounds,
Or memorize another Golgotha,

I cannot tell: but I am faint,
My Gashes cry for helpe

King. So well thy words become thee, as thy wounds,
They smack of Honor both: Goe get him Surgeons.
Enter Rosse and Angus.

Who comes here?
  Mal. The worthy Thane of Rosse

  Lenox. What a haste lookes through his eyes?
So should he looke, that seemes to speake things strange

Rosse. God saue the King

  King. Whence cam'st thou, worthy Thane?
  Rosse. From Fiffe, great King,
Where the Norweyan Banners flowt the Skie,
And fanne our people cold.
Norway himselfe, with terrible numbers,
Assisted by that most disloyall Traytor,
The Thane of Cawdor, began a dismall Conflict,
Till that Bellona's Bridegroome, lapt in proofe,
Confronted him with selfe-comparisons,
Point against Point, rebellious Arme 'gainst Arme,
Curbing his lauish spirit: and to conclude,
The Victorie fell on vs

King. Great happinesse

  Rosse. That now Sweno, the Norwayes King,
Craues composition:
Nor would we deigne him buriall of his men,
Till he disbursed, at Saint Colmes ynch,
Ten thousand Dollars, to our generall vse

  King. No more that Thane of Cawdor shall deceiue
Our Bosome interest: Goe pronounce his present death,
And with his former Title greet Macbeth

Rosse. Ile see it done

King. What he hath lost, Noble Macbeth hath wonne.

Exeunt.

Scena Tertia.

Thunder. Enter the three Witches.

    1. Where hast thou beene, Sister? 2. Killing Swine

  3. Sister, where thou?
  1. A Saylors Wife had Chestnuts in her Lappe,
And mouncht, & mouncht, and mouncht:
Giue me, quoth I.
Aroynt thee, Witch, the rumpe-fed Ronyon cryes.
Her Husband's to Aleppo gone, Master o'th' Tiger:
But in a Syue Ile thither sayle,
And like a Rat without a tayle,
Ile doe, Ile doe, and Ile doe

2. Ile giue thee a Winde

1. Th'art kinde

3. And I another

  1. I my selfe haue all the other,
And the very Ports they blow,
All the Quarters that they know,
I'th' Ship-mans Card.
Ile dreyne him drie as Hay:
Sleepe shall neyther Night nor Day
Hang vpon his Pent-house Lid:
He shall liue a man forbid:
Wearie Seu'nights, nine times nine,
Shall he dwindle, peake, and pine:
Though his Barke cannot be lost,
Yet it shall be Tempest-tost.
Looke what I haue

2. Shew me, shew me

1. Here I haue a Pilots Thumbe, Wrackt, as homeward he did come.

Drum within.

3. A Drumme, a Drumme:
Macbeth doth come

  All. The weyward Sisters, hand in hand,
Posters of the Sea and Land,
Thus doe goe, about, about,
Thrice to thine, and thrice to mine,
And thrice againe, to make vp nine.
Peace, the Charme's wound vp.
Enter Macbeth and Banquo.

Macb. So foule and faire a day I haue not seene

  Banquo. How farre is't call'd to Soris? What are these,
So wither'd, and so wilde in their attyre,
That looke not like th' Inhabitants o'th' Earth,
And yet are on't? Liue you, or are you aught
That man may question? you seeme to vnderstand me,
By each at once her choppie finger laying
Vpon her skinnie Lips: you should be Women,
And yet your Beards forbid me to interprete
That you are so

  Mac. Speake if you can: what are you?
  1. All haile Macbeth, haile to thee Thane of Glamis

2. All haile Macbeth, haile to thee Thane of Cawdor

3. All haile Macbeth, that shalt be King hereafter

  Banq. Good Sir, why doe you start, and seeme to feare
Things that doe sound so faire? i'th' name of truth
Are ye fantasticall, or that indeed
Which outwardly ye shew? My Noble Partner
You greet with present Grace, and great prediction
Of Noble hauing, and of Royall hope,

That he seemes wrapt withall: to me you speake not.
If you can looke into the Seedes of Time,
And say, which Graine will grow, and which will not,
Speake then to me, who neyther begge, nor feare
Your fauors, nor your hate

1. Hayle

2. Hayle

3. Hayle

1. Lesser than Macbeth, and greater

2. Not so happy, yet much happyer

> 3. Thou shalt get Kings, though thou be none: So all haile
> Macbeth, and Banquo

1. Banquo, and Macbeth, all haile

  Macb. Stay you imperfect Speakers, tell me more:
By Sinells death, I know I am Thane of Glamis,
But how, of Cawdor? the Thane of Cawdor liues
A prosperous Gentleman: And to be King,
Stands not within the prospect of beleefe,
No more then to be Cawdor. Say from whence
You owe this strange Intelligence, or why
Vpon this blasted Heath you stop our way
With such Prophetique greeting?
Speake, I charge you.

Witches vanish.

  Banq. The Earth hath bubbles, as the Water ha's,
And these are of them: whither are they vanish'd?
  Macb. Into the Ayre: and what seem'd corporall,
Melted, as breath into the Winde.
Would they had stay'd

  Banq. Were such things here, as we doe speake about?
Or haue we eaten on the insane Root,

That takes the Reason Prisoner?
  Macb. Your Children shall be Kings

Banq. You shall be King

  Macb. And Thane of Cawdor too: went it not so?
  Banq. Toth' selfe-same tune and words: who's here?
Enter Rosse and Angus.

  Rosse. The King hath happily receiu'd, Macbeth,
The newes of thy successe: and when he reades
Thy personall Venture in the Rebels sight,
His Wonders and his Prayses doe contend,
Which should be thine, or his: silenc'd with that,
In viewing o're the rest o'th' selfe-same day,
He findes thee in the stout Norweyan Rankes,
Nothing afeard of what thy selfe didst make
Strange Images of death, as thick as Tale
Can post with post, and euery one did beare
Thy prayses in his Kingdomes great defence,
And powr'd them downe before him

  Ang. Wee are sent,
To giue thee from our Royall Master thanks,
Onely to harrold thee into his sight,
Not pay thee

  Rosse. And for an earnest of a greater Honor,
He bad me, from him, call thee Thane of Cawdor:
In which addition, haile most worthy Thane,
For it is thine

  Banq. What, can the Deuill speake true?
  Macb. The Thane of Cawdor liues:
Why doe you dresse me in borrowed Robes?
  Ang. Who was the Thane, liues yet,
But vnder heauie Iudgement beares that Life,
Which he deserues to loose.
Whether he was combin'd with those of Norway,
Or did lyne the Rebell with hidden helpe,

And vantage; or that with both he labour'd
In his Countreyes wracke, I know not:
But Treasons Capitall, confess'd, and prou'd,
Haue ouerthrowne him

  Macb. Glamys, and Thane of Cawdor:
The greatest is behinde. Thankes for your paines.
Doe you not hope your Children shall be Kings,
When those that gaue the Thane of Cawdor to me,
Promis'd no lesse to them

  Banq. That trusted home,
Might yet enkindle you vnto the Crowne,
Besides the Thane of Cawdor. But 'tis strange:
And oftentimes, to winne vs to our harme,
The Instruments of Darknesse tell vs Truths,
Winne vs with honest Trifles, to betray's
In deepest consequence.
Cousins, a word, I pray you

  Macb. Two Truths are told,
As happy Prologues to the swelling Act
Of the Imperiall Theame. I thanke you Gentlemen:
This supernaturall solliciting
Cannot be ill; cannot be good.
If ill? why hath it giuen me earnest of successe,
Commencing in a Truth? I am Thane of Cawdor.
If good? why doe I yeeld to that suggestion,
Whose horrid Image doth vnfixe my Heire,
And make my seated Heart knock at my Ribbes,
Against the vse of Nature? Present Feares
Are lesse then horrible Imaginings:
My Thought, whose Murther yet is but fantasticall,
Shakes so my single state of Man,
That Function is smother'd in surmise,
And nothing is, but what is not

Banq. Looke how our Partner's rapt

Macb. If Chance will haue me King,
Why Chance may Crowne me,
Without my stirre

Banq. New Honors come vpon him
Like our strange Garments, cleaue not to their mould,
But with the aid of vse

Macb. Come what come may,
Time, and the Houre, runs through the roughest Day

Banq. Worthy Macbeth, wee stay vpon your leysure

Macb. Giue me your fauour:
My dull Braine was wrought with things forgotten.
Kinde Gentlemen, your paines are registred,
Where euery day I turne the Leafe,
To reade them.
Let vs toward the King: thinke vpon
What hath chanc'd: and at more time,
The Interim hauing weigh'd it, let vs speake
Our free Hearts each to other

Banq. Very gladly

Macb. Till then enough:
Come friends.

Exeunt.

Scena Quarta.

Flourish. Enter King, Lenox, Malcolme, Donalbaine, and
Attendants.

King. Is execution done on Cawdor?
Or not those in Commission yet return'd?
Mal. My Liege, they are not yet come back.
But I haue spoke with one that saw him die:
Who did report, that very frankly hee
Confess'd his Treasons, implor'd your Highnesse Pardon,

And set forth a deepe Repentance:
Nothing in his Life became him,
Like the leauing it. Hee dy'de,
As one that had beene studied in his death,
To throw away the dearest thing he ow'd,
As 'twere a carelesse Trifle

   King. There's no Art,
To finde the Mindes construction in the Face.
He was a Gentleman, on whom I built
An absolute Trust.
Enter Macbeth, Banquo, Rosse, and Angus.

O worthyest Cousin,
The sinne of my Ingratitude euen now
Was heauie on me. Thou art so farre before,
That swiftest Wing of Recompence is slow,
To ouertake thee. Would thou hadst lesse deseru'd,
That the proportion both of thanks, and payment,
Might haue beene mine: onely I haue left to say,
More is thy due, then more then all can pay

   Macb. The seruice, and the loyaltie I owe,
In doing it, payes it selfe.
Your Highnesse part, is to receiue our Duties:
And our Duties are to your Throne, and State,
Children, and Seruants; which doe but what they should,
By doing euery thing safe toward your Loue
And Honor

   King. Welcome hither:
I haue begun to plant thee, and will labour
To make thee full of growing. Noble Banquo,
That hast no lesse deseru'd, nor must be knowne
No lesse to haue done so: Let me enfold thee,
And hold thee to my Heart

   Banq. There if I grow,
The Haruest is your owne

King. My plenteous Ioyes,
Wanton in fulnesse, seeke to hide themselues
In drops of sorrow. Sonnes, Kinsmen, Thanes,
And you whose places are the nearest, know,
We will establish our Estate vpon
Our eldest, Malcolme, whom we name hereafter,
The Prince of Cumberland: which Honor must
Not vnaccompanied, inuest him onely,
But signes of Noblenesse, like Starres, shall shine
On all deseruers. From hence to Envernes,
And binde vs further to you

Macb. The Rest is Labor, which is not vs'd for you:
Ile be my selfe the Herbenger, and make ioyfull
The hearing of my Wife, with your approach:
So humbly take my leaue

King. My worthy Cawdor

Macb. The Prince of Cumberland: that is a step,
On which I must fall downe, or else o're-leape,
For in my way it lyes. Starres hide your fires,
Let not Light see my black and deepe desires:
The Eye winke at the Hand: yet let that bee,
Which the Eye feares, when it is done to see.
Enter.

King. True worthy Banquo: he is full so valiant,
And in his commendations, I am fed:
It is a Banquet to me. Let's after him,
Whose care is gone before, to bid vs welcome:
It is a peerelesse Kinsman.

Flourish. Exeunt.

Scena Quinta.

Enter Macbeths Wife alone with a Letter.

Lady. They met me in the day of successe: and I haue learn'd by the perfect'st report, they haue more in them, then mortall knowledge. When I burnt in desire to question them further, they made themselues Ayre, into which they vanish'd. Whiles I stood rapt in the wonder of it, came Missiues from the King, who all-hail'd me Thane of Cawdor, by which Title before, these weyward Sisters saluted me, and referr'd me to the comming on of time, with haile King that shalt be. This haue I thought good to deliuer thee (my dearest Partner of Greatnesse) that thou might'st not loose the dues of reioycing by being ignorant of what Greatnesse is promis'd thee. Lay it to thy heart and farewell. Glamys thou art, and Cawdor, and shalt be What thou art promis'd: yet doe I feare thy Nature, It is too full o'th' Milke of humane kindnesse, To catch the neerest way. Thou would'st be great, Art not without Ambition, but without The illnesse should attend it. What thou would'st highly, That would'st thou holily: would'st not play false, And yet would'st wrongly winne. Thould'st haue, great Glamys, that which cryes, Thus thou must doe, if thou haue it; And that which rather thou do'st feare to doe, Then wishest should be vndone. High thee hither, That I may powre my Spirits in thine Eare, And chastise with the valour of my Tongue All that impeides thee from the Golden Round, Which Fate and Metaphysicall ayde doth seeme To haue thee crown'd withall. Enter Messenger.

What is your tidings?
  Mess. The King comes here to Night

  Lady. Thou'rt mad to say it.
Is not thy Master with him? who, wer't so,
Would haue inform'd for preparation

  Mess. So please you, it is true: our Thane is comming:
One of my fellowes had the speed of him;
Who almost dead for breath, had scarcely more
Then would make vp his Message

  Lady. Giue him tending,
He brings great newes,

Exit Messenger.

The Rauen himselfe is hoarse,
That croakes the fatall entrance of Duncan
Vnder my Battlements. Come you Spirits,
That tend on mortall thoughts, vnsex me here,
And fill me from the Crowne to the Toe, top-full
Of direst Crueltie: make thick my blood,
Stop vp th' accesse, and passage to Remorse,
That no compunctious visitings of Nature
Shake my fell purpose, nor keepe peace betweene
Th' effect, and hit. Come to my Womans Brests,
And take my Milke for Gall, you murth'ring Ministers,
Where-euer, in your sightlesse substances,
You wait on Natures Mischiefe. Come thick Night,
And pall thee in the dunnest smoake of Hell,

That my keene Knife see not the Wound it makes,
Nor Heauen peepe through the Blanket of the darke,
To cry, hold, hold.
Enter Macbeth.

Great Glamys, worthy Cawdor,
Greater then both, by the all-haile hereafter,
Thy Letters haue transported me beyond
This ignorant present, and I feele now
The future in the instant

   Macb. My dearest Loue,
Duncan comes here to Night

   Lady. And when goes hence?
   Macb. To morrow, as he purposes

   Lady. O neuer,
Shall Sunne that Morrow see.
Your Face, my Thane, is as a Booke, where men
May reade strange matters, to beguile the time.
Looke like the time, beare welcome in your Eye,
Your Hand, your Tongue: looke like th' innocent flower,
But be the Serpent vnder't. He that's comming,
Must be prouided for: and you shall put

This Nights great Businesse into my dispatch,
Which shall to all our Nights, and Dayes to come,
Giue solely soueraigne sway, and Masterdome

  Macb. We will speake further,
  Lady. Onely looke vp cleare:
To alter fauor, euer is to feare:
Leaue all the rest to me.

Exeunt.

Scena Sexta.

Hoboyes, and Torches. Enter King, Malcolme, Donalbaine,
Banquo, Lenox,
Macduff, Rosse, Angus, and Attendants.

  King. This Castle hath a pleasant seat,
The ayre nimbly and sweetly recommends it selfe
Vnto our gentle sences

  Banq. This Guest of Summer,
The Temple-haunting Barlet does approue,
By his loued Mansonry, that the Heauens breath
Smells wooingly here: no Iutty frieze,
Buttrice, nor Coigne of Vantage, but this Bird
Hath made his pendant Bed, and procreant Cradle,
Where they must breed, and haunt: I haue obseru'd
The ayre is delicate.
Enter Lady.

  King. See, see our honor'd Hostesse:
The Loue that followes vs, sometime is our trouble,
Which still we thanke as Loue. Herein I teach you,
How you shall bid God-eyld vs for your paines,
And thanke vs for your trouble

  Lady. All our seruice,
In euery point twice done, and then done double,
Were poore, and single Businesse, to contend

Against those Honors deepe, and broad,
Wherewith your Maiestie loades our House:
For those of old, and the late Dignities,
Heap'd vp to them, we rest your Ermites

   King. Where's the Thane of Cawdor?
We courst him at the heeles, and had a purpose
To be his Purueyor: But he rides well,
And his great Loue (sharpe as his Spurre) hath holp him
To his home before vs: Faire and Noble Hostesse
We are your guest to night

   La. Your Seruants euer,
Haue theirs, themselues, and what is theirs in compt,
To make their Audit at your Highnesse pleasure,
Still to returne your owne

   King. Giue me your hand:
Conduct me to mine Host we loue him highly,
And shall continue, our Graces towards him.
By your leaue Hostesse.

Exeunt.

Scena Septima.

Hoboyes. Torches. Enter a Sewer, and diuers Seruants with Dishes and
Seruice ouer the Stage. Then enter Macbeth

   Macb. If it were done, when 'tis done, then 'twer well,
It were done quickly: If th' Assassination
Could trammell vp the Consequence, and catch
With his surcease, Successe: that but this blow
Might be the be all, and the end all. Heere,
But heere, vpon this Banke and Schoole of time,
Wee'ld iumpe the life to come. But in these Cases,
We still haue iudgement heere, that we but teach
Bloody Instructions, which being taught, returne
To plague th' Inuenter, this euen-handed Iustice
Commends th' Ingredience of our poyson'd Challice

To our owne lips. Hee's heere in double trust;
First, as I am his Kinsman, and his Subiect,
Strong both against the Deed: Then, as his Host,
Who should against his Murtherer shut the doore,
Not beare the knife my selfe. Besides, this Duncane
Hath borne his Faculties so meeke; hath bin
So cleere in his great Office, that his Vertues
Will pleade like Angels, Trumpet-tongu'd against
The deepe damnation of his taking off:
And Pitty, like a naked New-borne-Babe,
Striding the blast, or Heauens Cherubin, hors'd
Vpon the sightlesse Curriors of the Ayre,
Shall blow the horrid deed in euery eye,
That teares shall drowne the winde. I haue no Spurre
To pricke the sides of my intent, but onely
Vaulting Ambition, which ore-leapes it selfe,
And falles on th' other.
Enter Lady.

How now? What Newes?
  La. He has almost supt: why haue you left the chamber?
  Mac. Hath he ask'd for me?
  La. Know you not, he ha's?
  Mac. We will proceed no further in this Businesse:
He hath Honour'd me of late, and I haue bought
Golden Opinions from all sorts of people,
Which would be worne now in their newest glosse,
Not cast aside so soone

   La. Was the hope drunke,
Wherein you drest your selfe? Hath it slept since?
And wakes it now to looke so greene, and pale,
At what it did so freely? From this time,
Such I account thy loue. Art thou affear'd
To be the same in thine owne Act, and Valour,
As thou art in desire? Would'st thou haue that
Which thou esteem'st the Ornament of Life,
And liue a Coward in thine owne Esteeme?

Letting I dare not, wait vpon I would,
Like the poore Cat i'th' Addage

  Macb. Prythee peace:
I dare do all that may become a man,
Who dares do more, is none

  La. What Beast was't then
That made you breake this enterprize to me?
When you durst do it, then you were a man:
And to be more then what you were, you would
Be so much more the man. Nor time, nor place
Did then adhere, and yet you would make both:
They haue made themselues, and that their fitnesse now
Do's vnmake you. I haue giuen Sucke, and know
How tender 'tis to loue the Babe that milkes me,
I would, while it was smyling in my Face,
Haue pluckt my Nipple from his Bonelesse Gummes,
And dasht the Braines out, had I so sworne
As you haue done to this

  Macb. If we should faile?
  Lady. We faile?
But screw your courage to the sticking place,
And wee'le not fayle: when Duncan is asleepe,
(Whereto the rather shall his dayes hard Iourney
Soundly inuite him) his two Chamberlaines
Will I with Wine, and Wassell, so conuince,
That Memorie, the Warder of the Braine,
Shall be a Fume, and the Receit of Reason
A Lymbeck onely: when in Swinish sleepe,
Their drenched Natures lyes as in a Death,
What cannot you and I performe vpon
Th' vnguarded Duncan? What not put vpon
His spungie Officers? who shall beare the guilt
Of our great quell

  Macb. Bring forth Men-Children onely:
For thy vndaunted Mettle should compose
Nothing but Males. Will it not be receiu'd,

When we haue mark'd with blood those sleepie two
Of his owne Chamber, and vs'd their very Daggers,
That they haue don't?
  Lady. Who dares receiue it other,
As we shall make our Griefes and Clamor rore,
Vpon his Death?
  Macb. I am settled, and bend vp
Each corporall Agent to this terrible Feat.
Away, and mock the time with fairest show,
False Face must hide what the false Heart doth know.

Exeunt.

Actus Secundus. Scena Prima.

Enter Banquo, and Fleance, with a Torch before him.

  Banq. How goes the Night, Boy?
  Fleance. The Moone is downe: I haue not heard the
Clock

Banq. And she goes downe at Twelue

Fleance. I take't, 'tis later, Sir

  Banq. Hold, take my Sword:
There's Husbandry in Heauen,
Their Candles are all out: take thee that too.
A heauie Summons lyes like Lead vpon me,
And yet I would not sleepe:
Mercifull Powers, restraine in me the cursed thoughts
That Nature giues way to in repose.
Enter Macbeth, and a Seruant with a Torch.

Giue me my Sword: who's there?
  Macb. A Friend

  Banq. What Sir, not yet at rest? the King's a bed.
He hath beene in vnusuall Pleasure,
And sent forth great Largesse to your Offices.

This Diamond he greetes your Wife withall,
By the name of most kind Hostesse,
And shut vp in measurelesse content

  Mac. Being vnprepar'd,
Our will became the seruant to defect,
Which else should free haue wrought

  Banq. All's well.
I dreamt last Night of the three weyward Sisters:
To you they haue shew'd some truth

  Macb. I thinke not of them:
Yet when we can entreat an houre to serue,
We would spend it in some words vpon that Businesse,
If you would graunt the time

Banq. At your kind'st leysure

  Macb. If you shall cleaue to my consent,
When 'tis, it shall make Honor for you

  Banq. So I lose none,
In seeking to augment it, but still keepe
My Bosome franchis'd, and Allegeance cleare,
I shall be counsail'd

Macb. Good repose the while

Banq. Thankes Sir: the like to you.

Exit Banquo.

  Macb. Goe bid thy Mistresse, when my drinke is ready,
She strike vpon the Bell. Get thee to bed.
Enter.

Is this a Dagger, which I see before me,
The Handle toward my Hand? Come, let me clutch thee:
I haue thee not, and yet I see thee still.
Art thou not fatall Vision, sensible
To feeling, as to sight? or art thou but

A Dagger of the Minde, a false Creation,
Proceeding from the heat-oppressed Braine?
I see thee yet, in forme as palpable,
As this which now I draw.
Thou marshall'st me the way that I was going,
And such an Instrument I was to vse.
Mine Eyes are made the fooles o'th' other Sences,
Or else worth all the rest: I see thee still;
And on thy Blade, and Dudgeon, Gouts of Blood,
Which was not so before. There's no such thing:
It is the bloody Businesse, which informes
Thus to mine Eyes. Now o're the one halfe World
Nature seemes dead, and wicked Dreames abuse
The Curtain'd sleepe: Witchcraft celebrates
Pale Heccats Offrings: and wither'd Murther,
Alarum'd by his Centinell, the Wolfe,
Whose howle's his Watch, thus with his stealthy pace,
With Tarquins rauishing sides, towards his designe
Moues like a Ghost. Thou sowre and firme-set Earth
Heare not my steps, which they may walke, for feare
Thy very stones prate of my where-about,
And take the present horror from the time,
Which now sutes with it. Whiles I threat, he liues:
Words to the heat of deedes too cold breath giues.

A Bell rings.

I goe, and it is done: the Bell inuites me.
Heare it not, Duncan, for it is a Knell,
That summons thee to Heauen, or to Hell.
Enter.

Scena Secunda.

Enter Lady.

  La. That which hath made the[m] drunk, hath made me bold:
What hath quench'd them, hath giuen me fire.
Hearke, peace: it was the Owle that shriek'd,

The fatall Bell-man, which giues the stern'st good-night.
He is about it, the Doores are open:
And the surfeted Groomes doe mock their charge
With Snores. I haue drugg'd their Possets,
That Death and Nature doe contend about them,
Whether they liue, or dye.
Enter Macbeth.

  Macb. Who's there? what hoa?
  Lady. Alack, I am afraid they haue awak'd,
And 'tis not done: th' attempt, and not the deed,
Confounds vs: hearke: I lay'd their Daggers ready,
He could not misse 'em. Had he not resembled
My Father as he slept, I had don't.
My Husband?
  Macb. I haue done the deed:
Didst thou not heare a noyse?
  Lady. I heard the Owle schreame, and the Crickets cry.
Did not you speake?
  Macb. When?
  Lady. Now

  Macb. As I descended?
  Lady. I

  Macb. Hearke, who lyes i'th' second Chamber?
  Lady. Donalbaine

Mac. This is a sorry sight

Lady. A foolish thought, to say a sorry sight

  Macb. There's one did laugh in's sleepe,
And one cry'd Murther, that they did wake each other:
I stood, and heard them: But they did say their Prayers,
And addrest them againe to sleepe

Lady. There are two lodg'd together

  Macb. One cry'd God blesse vs, and Amen the other,
As they had seene me with these Hangmans hands:

Listning their feare, I could not say Amen,
When they did say God blesse vs

Lady. Consider it not so deepely

  Mac. But wherefore could not I pronounce Amen?
I had most need of Blessing, and Amen stuck in my throat

  Lady. These deeds must not be thought
After these wayes: so, it will make vs mad

  Macb. Me thought I heard a voyce cry, Sleep no more:
Macbeth does murther Sleepe, the innocent Sleepe,
Sleepe that knits vp the rauel'd Sleeue of Care,
The death of each dayes Life, sore Labors Bath,
Balme of hurt Mindes, great Natures second Course,
Chiefe nourisher in Life's Feast

  Lady. What doe you meane?
  Macb. Still it cry'd, Sleepe no more to all the House:
Glamis hath murther'd Sleepe, and therefore Cawdor
Shall sleepe no more: Macbeth shall sleepe no more

  Lady. Who was it, that thus cry'd? why worthy Thane,
You doe vnbend your Noble strength, to thinke
So braine-sickly of things: Goe get some Water,
And wash this filthie Witnesse from your Hand.
Why did you bring these Daggers from the place?
They must lye there: goe carry them, and smeare
The sleepie Groomes with blood

  Macb. Ile goe no more:
I am afraid, to thinke what I haue done:
Looke on't againe, I dare not

  Lady. Infirme of purpose:
Giue me the Daggers: the sleeping, and the dead,
Are but as Pictures: 'tis the Eye of Childhood,
That feares a painted Deuill. If he doe bleed,
Ile guild the Faces of the Groomes withall,

For it must seeme their Guilt.
Enter.

Knocke within.

  Macb. Whence is that knocking?
How is't with me, when euery noyse appalls me?
What Hands are here? hah: they pluck out mine Eyes.
Will all great Neptunes Ocean wash this blood
Cleane from my Hand? no: this my Hand will rather
The multitudinous Seas incarnardine,
Making the Greene one, Red.
Enter Lady.

  Lady. My Hands are of your colour: but I shame
To weare a Heart so white.

Knocke.

I heare a knocking at the South entry:
Retyre we to our Chamber:
A little Water cleares vs of this deed.
How easie is it then? your Constancie
Hath left you vnattended.

Knocke.

Hearke, more knocking.
Get on your Night-Gowne, least occasion call vs,
And shew vs to be Watchers: be not lost
So poorely in your thoughts

Macb. To know my deed,

Knocke.

'Twere best not know my selfe.
Wake Duncan with thy knocking:
I would thou could'st.

Exeunt.

Scena Tertia.

Enter a Porter. Knocking within.

  Porter. Here's a knocking indeede: if a man were
Porter of Hell Gate, hee should haue old turning the
Key.

Knock.

Knock, Knock, Knock. Who's there i'th' name of Belzebub? Here's a
Farmer, that hang'd himselfe on th' expectation of Plentie: Come in
time, haue Napkins enow about you, here you'le sweat for't.

Knock.

Knock, knock. Who's there in th' other Deuils Name? Faith here's an
Equiuocator, that could sweare in both the Scales against eyther Scale,
who committed Treason enough for Gods sake, yet could not
equiuocate to Heauen: oh come in, Equiuocator.

Knock.

Knock, Knock, Knock. Who's there? 'Faith here's an English
Taylor come hither, for stealing out of a French Hose:
Come in Taylor, here you may rost your Goose.
Knock.

Knock, Knock. Neuer at quiet: What are you? but this place is too cold
for Hell. Ile Deuill-Porter it no further: I had thought to haue let in
some of all Professions, that goe the Primrose way to th' euerlasting
Bonfire.

Knock.

Anon, anon, I pray you remember the Porter.
Enter Macduff, and Lenox.

  Macd. Was it so late, friend, ere you went to Bed,
That you doe lye so late?
  Port. Faith Sir, we were carowsing till the second Cock:
And Drinke, Sir, is a great prouoker of three things

Macd. What three things does Drinke especially prouoke? Port. Marry, Sir, Nose-painting, Sleepe, and Vrine. Lecherie, Sir, it prouokes, and vnprouokes: it prouokes the desire, but it takes away the performance. Therefore much Drinke may be said to be an Equiuocator with Lecherie: it makes him, and it marres him; it sets him on, and it takes him off; it perswades him, and dis-heartens him; makes him stand too, and not stand too: in conclusion, equiuocates him in a sleepe, and giuing him the Lye, leaues him

Macd. I beleeue, Drinke gaue thee the Lye last Night

Port. That it did, Sir, i'the very Throat on me: but I requited him for his Lye, and (I thinke) being too strong for him, though he tooke vp my Legges sometime, yet I made a Shift to cast him. Enter Macbeth.

  Macd. Is thy Master stirring?
Our knocking ha's awak'd him: here he comes

Lenox. Good morrow, Noble Sir

Macb. Good morrow both

  Macd. Is the King stirring, worthy Thane?
  Macb. Not yet

  Macd. He did command me to call timely on him,
I haue almost slipt the houre

Macb. Ile bring you to him

  Macd. I know this is a ioyfull trouble to you:
But yet 'tis one

  Macb. The labour we delight in, Physicks paine:
This is the Doore

  Macd. Ile make so bold to call, for 'tis my limitted seruice.

Exit Macduffe.

  Lenox. Goes the King hence to day?
  Macb. He does: he did appoint so

Lenox. The Night ha's been vnruly:
Where we lay, our Chimneys were blowne downe,
And (as they say) lamentings heard i'th' Ayre;
Strange Schreemes of Death,
And Prophecying, with Accents terrible,
Of dyre Combustion, and confus'd Euents,
New hatch'd toth' wofull time.
The obscure Bird clamor'd the liue-long Night.
Some say, the Earth was Feuorous,
And did shake

Macb. 'Twas a rough Night

Lenox. My young remembrance cannot paralell
A fellow to it.
Enter Macduff.

Macd. O horror, horror, horror,
Tongue nor Heart cannot conceiue, nor name thee

Macb. and Lenox. What's the matter?
Macd. Confusion now hath made his Master-peece:
Most sacrilegious Murther hath broke ope
The Lords anoynted Temple, and stole thence
The Life o'th' Building

Macb. What is't you say, the Life?
Lenox. Meane you his Maiestie?
Macd. Approch the Chamber, and destroy your sight
With a new Gorgon. Doe not bid me speake:
See, and then speake your selues: awake, awake,

Exeunt. Macbeth and Lenox.

Ring the Alarum Bell: Murther, and Treason,
Banquo, and Donalbaine: Malcolme awake,
Shake off this Downey sleepe, Deaths counterfeit,
And looke on Death it selfe: vp, vp, and see
The great Doomes Image: Malcolme, Banquo,
As from your Graues rise vp, and walke like Sprights,
To countenance this horror. Ring the Bell.

Bell rings. Enter Lady.

Lady. What's the Businesse?
That such a hideous Trumpet calls to parley
The sleepers of the House? speake, speake

Macd. O gentle Lady,
'Tis not for you to heare what I can speake:
The repetition in a Womans eare,
Would murther as it fell.
Enter Banquo.

O Banquo, Banquo, Our Royall Master's murther'd

Lady. Woe, alas:
What, in our House?
Ban. Too cruell, any where.
Deare Duff, I prythee contradict thy selfe,
And say, it is not so.
Enter Macbeth, Lenox, and Rosse.

Macb. Had I but dy'd an houre before this chance,
I had liu'd a blessed time: for from this instant,
There's nothing serious in Mortalitie:
All is but Toyes: Renowne and Grace is dead,
The Wine of Life is drawne, and the meere Lees
Is left this Vault, to brag of.
Enter Malcolme and Donalbaine.

Donal. What is amisse?
Macb. You are, and doe not know't:
The Spring, the Head, the Fountaine of your Blood
Is stopt, the very Source of it is stopt

Macd. Your Royall Father's murther'd

Mal. Oh, by whom?
Lenox. Those of his Chamber, as it seem'd, had don't:
Their Hands and Faces were all badg'd with blood,
So were their Daggers, which vnwip'd, we found

Vpon their Pillowes: they star'd, and were distracted,
No mans Life was to be trusted with them

  Macb. O, yet I doe repent me of my furie,
That I did kill them

  Macd. Wherefore did you so?
  Macb. Who can be wise, amaz'd, temp'rate, & furious,
Loyall, and Neutrall, in a moment? No man:
Th' expedition of my violent Loue
Out-run the pawser, Reason. Here lay Duncan,
His Siluer skinne, lac'd with His Golden Blood,
And his gash'd Stabs, look'd like a Breach in Nature,
For Ruines wastfull entrance: there the Murtherers,
Steep'd in the Colours of their Trade; their Daggers
Vnmannerly breech'd with gore: who could refraine,
That had a heart to loue; and in that heart,
Courage, to make's loue knowne?
  Lady. Helpe me hence, hoa

Macd. Looke to the Lady

  Mal. Why doe we hold our tongues,
That most may clayme this argument for ours?
  Donal. What should be spoken here,
Where our Fate hid in an augure hole,
May rush, and seize vs? Let's away,
Our Teares are not yet brew'd

  Mal. Nor our strong Sorrow
Vpon the foot of Motion

  Banq. Looke to the Lady:
And when we haue our naked Frailties hid,
That suffer in exposure; let vs meet,
And question this most bloody piece of worke,
To know it further. Feares and scruples shake vs:
In the great Hand of God I stand, and thence,
Against the vndivulg'd pretence, I fight
Of Treasonous Mallice

Macd. And so doe I

All. So all

  Macb. Let's briefely put on manly readinesse,
And meet i'th' Hall together

All. Well contented.

Exeunt.

  Malc. What will you doe?
Let's not consort with them:
To shew an vnfelt Sorrow, is an Office
Which the false man do's easie.
Ile to England

  Don. To Ireland, I:
Our seperated fortune shall keepe vs both the safer:
Where we are, there's Daggers in mens smiles;
The neere in blood, the neerer bloody

  Malc. This murtherous Shaft that's shot,
Hath not yet lighted: and our safest way,
Is to auoid the ayme. Therefore to Horse,
And let vs not be daintie of leaue-taking,
But shift away: there's warrant in that Theft,
Which steales it selfe, when there's no mercie left.

Exeunt.

Scena Quarta.

Enter Rosse, with an Old man.

  Old man. Threescore and ten I can remember well,
Within the Volume of which Time, I haue seene
Houres dreadfull, and things strange: but this sore Night
Hath trifled former knowings

Rosse. Ha, good Father,
Thou seest the Heauens, as troubled with mans Act,
Threatens his bloody Stage: byth' Clock 'tis Day,
And yet darke Night strangles the trauailing Lampe:
Is't Nights predominance, or the Dayes shame,
That Darknesse does the face of Earth intombe,
When liuing Light should kisse it?
  Old man. 'Tis vnnaturall,
Euen like the deed that's done: On Tuesday last,
A Faulcon towring in her pride of place,
Was by a Mowsing Owle hawkt at, and kill'd

  Rosse. And Duncans Horses,
(A thing most strange, and certaine)
Beauteous, and swift, the Minions of their Race,
Turn'd wilde in nature, broke their stalls, flong out,
Contending 'gainst Obedience, as they would
Make Warre with Mankinde

Old man. 'Tis said, they eate each other

  Rosse. They did so:
To th' amazement of mine eyes that look'd vpon't.
Enter Macduffe.

Heere comes the good Macduffe.
How goes the world Sir, now?
  Macd. Why see you not?
  Ross. Is't known who did this more then bloody deed?
  Macd. Those that Macbeth hath slaine

  Ross. Alas the day,
What good could they pretend?
  Macd. They were subborned,
Malcolme, and Donalbaine the Kings two Sonnes
Are stolne away and fled, which puts vpon them
Suspition of the deed

  Rosse. 'Gainst Nature still,
Thriftlesse Ambition, that will rauen vp

Thine owne liues meanes: Then 'tis most like,
The Soueraignty will fall vpon Macbeth

  Macd. He is already nam'd, and gone to Scone
To be inuested

  Rosse. Where is Duncans body?
  Macd. Carried to Colmekill,
The Sacred Store-house of his Predecessors,
And Guardian of their Bones

  Rosse. Will you to Scone?
  Macd. No Cosin, Ile to Fife

Rosse. Well, I will thither

  Macd. Well may you see things wel done there: Adieu
Least our old Robes sit easier then our new

Rosse. Farewell, Father

  Old M. Gods benyson go with you, and with those
That would make good of bad, and Friends of Foes.

Exeunt. omnes

Actus Tertius. Scena Prima.

Enter Banquo.

  Banq. Thou hast it now, King, Cawdor, Glamis, all,
As the weyard Women promis'd, and I feare
Thou playd'st most fowly for't: yet it was saide
It should not stand in thy Posterity,
But that my selfe should be the Roote, and Father
Of many Kings. If there come truth from them,
As vpon thee Macbeth, their Speeches shine,
Why by the verities on thee made good,
May they not be my Oracles as well,
And set me vp in hope. But hush, no more.

Senit sounded. Enter Macbeth as King, Lady Lenox, Rosse, Lords, and
Attendants.

Macb. Heere's our chiefe Guest

   La. If he had beene forgotten,
It had bene as a gap in our great Feast,
And all-thing vnbecomming

   Macb. To night we hold a solemne Supper sir,
And Ile request your presence

   Banq. Let your Highnesse
Command vpon me, to the which my duties
Are with a most indissoluble tye
For euer knit

   Macb. Ride you this afternoone?
   Ban. I, my good Lord

   Macb. We should haue else desir'd your good aduice
(Which still hath been both graue, and prosperous)
In this dayes Councell: but wee'le take to morrow.
Is't farre you ride?
   Ban. As farre, my Lord, as will fill vp the time
'Twixt this, and Supper. Goe not my Horse the better,
I must become a borrower of the Night,
For a darke houre, or twaine

Macb. Faile not our Feast

Ban. My Lord, I will not

   Macb. We heare our bloody Cozens are bestow'd
In England, and in Ireland, not confessing
Their cruell Parricide, filling their hearers
With strange inuention. But of that to morrow,
When therewithall, we shall haue cause of State,
Crauing vs ioyntly. Hye you to Horse:
Adieu, till you returne at Night.

Goes Fleance with you?
  Ban. I, my good Lord: our time does call vpon's

  Macb. I wish your Horses swift, and sure of foot:
And so I doe commend you to their backs.
Farwell.

Exit Banquo.

Let euery man be master of his time,
Till seuen at Night, to make societie
The sweeter welcome:
We will keepe our selfe till Supper time alone:
While then, God be with you.

Exeunt. Lords.

Sirrha, a word with you: Attend those men
Our pleasure?
  Seruant. They are, my Lord, without the Pallace
Gate

Macb. Bring them before vs.

Exit Seruant.

To be thus, is nothing, but to be safely thus
Our feares in Banquo sticke deepe,
And in his Royaltie of Nature reignes that
Which would be fear'd. 'Tis much he dares,
And to that dauntlesse temper of his Minde,
He hath a Wisdome, that doth guide his Valour,
To act in safetie. There is none but he,
Whose being I doe feare: and vnder him,
My Genius is rebuk'd, as it is said
Mark Anthonies was by Caesar. He chid the Sisters,
When first they put the Name of King vpon me,
And bad them speake to him. Then Prophet-like,
They hayl'd him Father to a Line of Kings.
Vpon my Head they plac'd a fruitlesse Crowne,
And put a barren Scepter in my Gripe,

Thence to be wrencht with an vnlineall Hand,
No Sonne of mine succeeding: if't be so,
For Banquo's Issue haue I fil'd my Minde,
For them, the gracious Duncan haue I murther'd,
Put Rancours in the Vessell of my Peace
Onely for them, and mine eternall Iewell
Giuen to the common Enemie of Man,
To make them Kings, the Seedes of Banquo Kings.
Rather then so, come Fate into the Lyst,
And champion me to th' vtterance.
Who's there?
Enter Seruant, and two Murtherers.

Now goe to the Doore, and stay there till we call.

Exit Seruant.

Was it not yesterday we spoke together?
  Murth. It was, so please your Highnesse

  Macb. Well then,
Now haue you consider'd of my speeches:
Know, that it was he, in the times past,
Which held you so vnder fortune,
Which you thought had been our innocent selfe.
This I made good to you, in our last conference,
Past in probation with you:
How you were borne in hand, how crost:
The Instruments: who wrought with them:
And all things else, that might
To halfe a Soule, and to a Notion craz'd,
Say, Thus did Banquo

1.Murth. You made it knowne to vs

  Macb. I did so:
And went further, which is now
Our point of second meeting.
Doe you finde your patience so predominant,
In your nature, that you can let this goe?

Are you so Gospell'd, to pray for this good man,
And for his Issue, whose heauie hand
Hath bow'd you to the Graue, and begger'd
Yours for euer?

  1.Murth. We are men, my Liege

  Macb. I, in the Catalogue ye goe for men,
As Hounds, and Greyhounds, Mungrels, Spaniels, Curres,
Showghes, Water-Rugs, and Demy-Wolues are clipt
All by the Name of Dogges: the valued file
Distinguishes the swift, the slow, the subtle,
The House-keeper, the Hunter, euery one
According to the gift, which bounteous Nature
Hath in him clos'd: whereby he does receiue
Particular addition, from the Bill,
That writes them all alike: and so of men.
Now, if you haue a station in the file,
Not i'th' worst ranke of Manhood, say't,
And I will put that Businesse in your Bosomes,
Whose execution takes your Enemie off,
Grapples you to the heart; and loue of vs,
Who weare our Health but sickly in his Life,
Which in his Death were perfect

  2.Murth. I am one, my Liege,
Whom the vile Blowes and Buffets of the World
Hath so incens'd, that I am recklesse what I doe,
To spight the World

  1.Murth. And I another,
So wearie with Disasters, tugg'd with Fortune,
That I would set my Life on any Chance,
To mend it, or be rid on't

Macb. Both of you know Banquo was your Enemie

Murth. True, my Lord

  Macb. So is he mine: and in such bloody distance,
That euery minute of his being, thrusts

Against my neer'st of Life: and though I could
With bare-fac'd power sweepe him from my sight,
And bid my will auouch it; yet I must not,
For certaine friends that are both his, and mine,
Whose loues I may not drop, but wayle his fall,
Who I my selfe struck downe: and thence it is,
That I to your assistance doe make loue,
Masking the Businesse from the common Eye,
For sundry weightie Reasons

  2.Murth. We shall, my Lord,
Performe what you command vs

  1.Murth. Though our Liues-
  Macb. Your Spirits shine through you.
Within this houre, at most,
I will aduise you where to plant your selues,
Acquaint you with the perfect Spy o'th' time,
The moment on't, for't must be done to Night,
And something from the Pallace: alwayes thought,
That I require a clearenesse; and with him,
To leaue no Rubs nor Botches in the Worke:
  Fleans , his Sonne, that keepes him companie,
Whose absence is no lesse materiall to me,
Then is his Fathers, must embrace the fate
Of that darke houre: resolue your selues apart,
Ile come to you anon

Murth. We are resolu'd, my Lord

  Macb. Ile call vpon you straight: abide within,
It is concluded: Banquo, thy Soules flight,
If it finde Heauen, must finde it out to Night.

Exeunt.

Scena Secunda.

Enter Macbeths Lady, and a Seruant.

Lady. Is Banquo gone from Court?

Seruant. I, Madame, but returnes againe to Night

Lady. Say to the King, I would attend his leysure,
For a few words

Seruant. Madame, I will.

Enter.

Lady. Nought's had, all's spent.
Where our desire is got without content:
'Tis safer, to be that which we destroy,
Then by destruction dwell in doubtfull ioy.

Enter Macbeth.

How now, my Lord, why doe you keepe alone?
Of sorryest Fancies your Companions making,
Vsing those Thoughts, which should indeed haue dy'd
With them they thinke on: things without all remedie
Should be without regard: what's done, is done

Macb. We haue scorch'd the Snake, not kill'd it:
Shee'le close, and be her selfe, whilest our poore Mallice
Remaines in danger of her former Tooth.
But let the frame of things dis-ioynt,
Both the Worlds suffer,
Ere we will eate our Meale in feare, and sleepe
In the affliction of these terrible Dreames,
That shake vs Nightly: Better be with the dead,
Whom we, to gayne our peace, haue sent to peace,
Then on the torture of the Minde to lye
In restlesse extasie.
Duncane is in his Graue:
After Lifes fitfull Feuer, he sleepes well,
Treason ha's done his worst: nor Steele, nor Poyson,
Mallice domestique, forraine Leuie, nothing,
Can touch him further

Lady. Come on:
Gentle my Lord, sleeke o're your rugged Lookes,
Be bright and Iouiall among your Guests to Night

Macb. So shall I Loue, and so I pray be you:
Let your remembrance apply to Banquo,
Present him Eminence, both with Eye and Tongue:
Vnsafe the while, that wee must laue
Our Honors in these flattering streames,
And make our Faces Vizards to our Hearts,
Disguising what they are

Lady. You must leaue this

Macb. O, full of Scorpions is my Minde, deare Wife:
Thou know'st, that Banquo and his Fleans liues

Lady. But in them, Natures Coppie's not eterne

Macb. There's comfort yet, they are assaileable,
Then be thou iocund: ere the Bat hath flowne
His Cloyster'd flight, ere to black Heccats summons
The shard-borne Beetle, with his drowsie hums,
Hath rung Nights yawning Peale,
There shall be done a deed of dreadfull note

Lady. What's to be done?
Macb. Be innocent of the knowledge, dearest Chuck,
Till thou applaud the deed: Come, seeling Night,
Skarfe vp the tender Eye of pittifull Day,
And with thy bloodie and inuisible Hand
Cancell and teare to pieces that great Bond,
Which keepes me pale. Light thickens,
And the Crow makes Wing toth' Rookie Wood:
Good things of Day begin to droope, and drowse,
Whiles Nights black Agents to their Prey's doe rowse.
Thou maruell'st at my words: but hold thee still,
Things bad begun, make strong themselues by ill:
So prythee goe with me.

Exeunt.

Scena Tertia.

Enter three Murtherers.

   1. But who did bid thee ioyne with vs? 3. Macbeth

2. He needes not our mistrust, since he deliuers Our Offices, and what we haue to doe, To the direction iust

   1. Then stand with vs:
The West yet glimmers with some streakes of Day.
Now spurres the lated Traueller apace,
To gayne the timely Inne, and neere approches
The subiect of our Watch

3. Hearke, I heare Horses

Banquo within. Giue vs a Light there, hoa

2. Then 'tis hee: The rest, that are within the note of expectation,
Alreadie are i'th' Court

1. His Horses goe about

   3. Almost a mile: but he does vsually,
So all men doe, from hence toth' Pallace Gate
Make it their Walke.
Enter Banquo and Fleans, with a Torch.

2. A Light, a Light

3. 'Tis hee

1. Stand too't

Ban. It will be Rayne to Night

1. Let it come downe

  Ban. O, Trecherie!
Flye good Fleans, flye, flye, flye,
Thou may'st reuenge. O Slaue!
  3. Who did strike out the Light?

1. Was't not the way?
3. There's but one downe: the Sonne is fled

 2. We haue lost
Best halfe of our Affaire

1. Well, let's away, and say how much is done.

Exeunt.

Scaena Quarta.

Banquet prepar'd. Enter Macbeth, Lady, Rosse, Lenox, Lords, and
Attendants.

  Macb. You know your owne degrees, sit downe:
At first and last, the hearty welcome

Lords. Thankes to your Maiesty

  Macb. Our selfe will mingle with Society,
And play the humble Host:
Our Hostesse keepes her State, but in best time
We will require her welcome

  La. Pronounce it for me Sir, to all our Friends,
For my heart speakes, they are welcome.
Enter first Murtherer.

  Macb. See they encounter thee with their harts thanks
Both sides are euen: heere Ile sit i'th' mid'st,
Be large in mirth, anon wee'l drinke a Measure
The Table round. There's blood vpon thy face

Mur. 'Tis Banquo's then

  Macb. 'Tis better thee without, then he within.
Is he dispatch'd?
  Mur. My Lord his throat is cut, that I did for him

Mac. Thou art the best o'th' Cut-throats,
Yet hee's good that did the like for Fleans:
If thou did'st it, thou art the Non-pareill

  Mur. Most Royall Sir
Fleans is scap'd

  Macb. Then comes my Fit againe:
I had else beene perfect;
Whole as the Marble, founded as the Rocke,
As broad, and generall, as the casing Ayre:
But now I am cabin'd, crib'd, confin'd, bound in
To sawcy doubts, and feares. But Banquo's safe?
  Mur. I, my good Lord: safe in a ditch he bides,
With twenty trenched gashes on his head;
The least a Death to Nature

  Macb. Thankes for that:
There the growne Serpent lyes, the worme that's fled
Hath Nature that in time will Venom breed,
No teeth for th' present. Get thee gone, to morrow
Wee'l heare our selues againe.

Exit Murderer.

  Lady. My Royall Lord,
You do not giue the Cheere, the Feast is sold
That is not often vouch'd, while 'tis a making:
'Tis giuen, with welcome: to feede were best at home:
From thence, the sawce to meate is Ceremony,
Meeting were bare without it.
Enter the Ghost of Banquo, and sits in Macbeths place.

  Macb. Sweet Remembrancer:
Now good digestion waite on Appetite,
And health on both

Lenox. May't please your Highnesse sit

  Macb. Here had we now our Countries Honor, roof'd,
Were the grac'd person of our Banquo present:

Who, may I rather challenge for vnkindnesse,
Then pitty for Mischance

  Rosse. His absence (Sir)
Layes blame vpon his promise. Pleas't your Highnesse
To grace vs with your Royall Company?
  Macb. The Table's full

Lenox. Heere is a place reseru'd Sir

  Macb. Where?
  Lenox. Heere my good Lord.
What is't that moues your Highnesse?
  Macb. Which of you haue done this?
  Lords. What, my good Lord?
  Macb. Thou canst not say I did it: neuer shake
Thy goary lockes at me

Rosse. Gentlemen rise, his Highnesse is not well

  Lady. Sit worthy Friends: my Lord is often thus,
And hath beene from his youth. Pray you keepe Seat,
The fit is momentary, vpon a thought
He will againe be well. If much you note him
You shall offend him, and extend his Passion,
Feed, and regard him not. Are you a man?
  Macb. I, and a bold one, that dare looke on that
Which might appall the Diuell

  La. O proper stuffe:
This is the very painting of your feare:
This is the Ayre-drawne-Dagger which you said
Led you to Duncan. O, these flawes and starts
(Impostors to true feare) would well become
A womans story, at a Winters fire
Authoriz'd by her Grandam: shame it selfe,
Why do you make such faces? When all's done
You looke but on a stoole

  Macb. Prythee see there:
Behold, looke, loe, how say you:

Why what care I, if thou canst nod, speake too.
If Charnell houses, and our Graues must send
Those that we bury, backe; our Monuments
Shall be the Mawes of Kytes

La. What? quite vnmann'd in folly

Macb. If I stand heere, I saw him

La. Fie for shame

  Macb. Blood hath bene shed ere now, i'th' olden time
Ere humane Statute purg'd the gentle Weale:
I, and since too, Murthers haue bene perform'd
Too terrible for the eare. The times has bene,
That when the Braines were out, the man would dye,
And there an end: But now they rise againe
With twenty mortall murthers on their crownes,
And push vs from our stooles. This is more strange
Then such a murther is

  La. My worthy Lord
Your Noble Friends do lacke you

  Macb. I do forget:
Do not muse at me my most worthy Friends,
I haue a strange infirmity, which is nothing
To those that know me. Come, loue and health to all,
Then Ile sit downe: Giue me some Wine, fill full:
Enter Ghost.

I drinke to th' generall ioy o'th' whole Table,
And to our deere Friend Banquo, whom we misse:
Would he were heere: to all, and him we thirst,
And all to all

Lords. Our duties, and the pledge

  Mac. Auant, & quit my sight, let the earth hide thee:
Thy bones are marrowlesse, thy blood is cold:

Thou hast no speculation in those eyes
Which thou dost glare with

La. Thinke of this good Peeres
But as a thing of Custome: 'Tis no other,
Onely it spoyles the pleasure of the time

Macb. What man dare, I dare:
Approach thou like the rugged Russian Beare,
The arm'd Rhinoceros, or th' Hircan Tiger,
Take any shape but that, and my firme Nerues
Shall neuer tremble. Or be aliue againe,
And dare me to the Desart with thy Sword:
If trembling I inhabit then, protest mee
The Baby of a Girle. Hence horrible shadow,
Vnreall mock'ry hence. Why so, being gone
I am a man againe: pray you sit still

La. You haue displac'd the mirth,
Broke the good meeting, with most admir'd disorder

Macb. Can such things be,
And ouercome vs like a Summers Clowd,
Without our speciall wonder? You make me strange
Euen to the disposition that I owe,
When now I thinke you can behold such sights,
And keepe the naturall Rubie of your Cheekes,
When mine is blanch'd with feare

Rosse. What sights, my Lord?
La. I pray you speake not: he growes worse & worse
Question enrages him: at once, goodnight.
Stand not vpon the order of your going,
But go at once

Len. Good night, and better health
Attend his Maiesty

La. A kinde goodnight to all.

Exit Lords.

Macb. It will haue blood they say:
Blood will haue Blood:
Stones haue beene knowne to moue, & Trees to speake:
Augures, and vnderstood Relations, haue
By Maggot Pyes, & Choughes, & Rookes brought forth
The secret'st man of Blood. What is the night?
  La. Almost at oddes with morning, which is which

  Macb. How say'st thou that Macduff denies his person
At our great bidding

  La. Did you send to him Sir?
  Macb. I heare it by the way: But I will send:
There's not a one of them but in his house
I keepe a Seruant Feed. I will to morrow
(And betimes I will) to the weyard Sisters.
More shall they speake: for now I am bent to know
By the worst meanes, the worst, for mine owne good,
All causes shall giue way. I am in blood
Stept in so farre, that should I wade no more,
Returning were as tedious as go ore:
Strange things I haue in head, that will to hand,
Which must be acted, ere they may be scand

La. You lacke the season of all Natures, sleepe

  Macb. Come, wee'l to sleepe: My strange & self-abuse
Is the initiate feare, that wants hard vse:
We are yet but yong indeed.

Exeunt.

Scena Quinta.

Thunder. Enter the three Witches, meeting Hecat.

  1. Why how now Hecat, you looke angerly?
  Hec. Haue I not reason (Beldams) as you are?
Sawcy, and ouer-bold, how did you dare
To Trade, and Trafficke with Macbeth,

In Riddles, and Affaires of death;
And I the Mistris of your Charmes,
The close contriuer of all harmes,
Was neuer call'd to beare my part,
Or shew the glory of our Art?
And which is worse, all you haue done
Hath bene but for a wayward Sonne,
Spightfull, and wrathfull, who (as others do)
Loues for his owne ends, not for you.
But make amends now: Get you gon,
And at the pit of Acheron
Meete me i'th' Morning: thither he
Will come, to know his Destinie.
Your Vessels, and your Spels prouide,
Your Charmes, and euery thing beside;
I am for th' Ayre: This night Ile spend
Vnto a dismall, and a Fatall end.
Great businesse must be wrought ere Noone.
Vpon the Corner of the Moone
There hangs a vap'rous drop, profound,
Ile catch it ere it come to ground;
And that distill'd by Magicke slights,
Shall raise such Artificiall Sprights,
As by the strength of their illusion,
Shall draw him on to his Confusion.
He shall spurne Fate, scorne Death, and beare
His hopes 'boue Wisedome, Grace, and Feare:
And you all know, Security
Is Mortals cheefest Enemie.

Musicke, and a Song.

Hearke, I am call'd: my little Spirit see
Sits in Foggy cloud, and stayes for me.

Sing within. Come away, come away, &c.

　　1 Come, let's make hast, shee'l soone be Backe againe.

Exeunt.

Scaena Sexta.

Enter Lenox, and another Lord.

Lenox. My former Speeches,
Haue but hit your Thoughts
Which can interpret farther: Onely I say
Things haue bin strangely borne. The gracious Duncan
Was pittied of Macbeth: marry he was dead:
And the right valiant Banquo walk'd too late,
Whom you may say (if't please you) Fleans kill'd,
For Fleans fled: Men must not walke too late.
Who cannot want the thought, how monstrous
It was for Malcolme, and for Donalbane
To kill their gracious Father? Damned Fact,
How it did greeue Macbeth? Did he not straight
In pious rage, the two delinquents teare,
That were the Slaues of drinke, and thralles of sleepe?
Was not that Nobly done? I, and wisely too:
For 'twould haue anger'd any heart aliue
To heare the men deny't. So that I say,
He ha's borne all things well, and I do thinke,
That had he Duncans Sonnes vnder his Key,
(As, and't please Heauen he shall not) they should finde
What 'twere to kill a Father: So should Fleans.
But peace; for from broad words, and cause he fayl'd
His presence at the Tyrants Feast, I heare
Macduffe liues in disgrace. Sir, can you tell
Where he bestowes himselfe?
Lord. The Sonnes of Duncane
(From whom this Tyrant holds the due of Birth)
Liues in the English Court, and is receyu'd
Of the most Pious Edward, with such grace,
That the maleuolence of Fortune, nothing
Takes from his high respect. Thither Macduffe
Is gone, to pray the Holy King, vpon his ayd
To wake Northumberland, and warlike Seyward,
That by the helpe of these (with him aboue)
To ratifie the Worke) we may againe

Giue to our Tables meate, sleepe to our Nights:
Free from our Feasts, and Banquets bloody kniues;
Do faithfull Homage, and receiue free Honors,
All which we pine for now. And this report
Hath so exasperate their King, that hee
Prepares for some attempt of Warre

   Len. Sent he to Macduffe?
  Lord. He did: and with an absolute Sir, not I
The clowdy Messenger turnes me his backe,
And hums; as who should say, you'l rue the time
That clogges me with this Answer

   Lenox. And that well might
Aduise him to a Caution, t' hold what distance
His wisedome can prouide. Some holy Angell
Flye to the Court of England, and vnfold
His Message ere he come, that a swift blessing
May soone returne to this our suffering Country,
Vnder a hand accurs'd

Lord. Ile send my Prayers with him.

Exeunt.

Actus Quartus. Scena Prima.

Thunder. Enter the three Witches.

1 Thrice the brinded Cat hath mew'd

2 Thrice, and once the Hedge-Pigge whin'd

3 Harpier cries, 'tis time, 'tis time

   1 Round about the Caldron go:
In the poysond Entrailes throw
Toad, that vnder cold stone,
Dayes and Nights, ha's thirty one:
Sweltred Venom sleeping got,
Boyle thou first i'th' charmed pot

All. Double, double, toile and trouble;
Fire burne, and Cauldron bubble

   2 Fillet of a Fenny Snake,
In the Cauldron boyle and bake:
Eye of Newt, and Toe of Frogge,
Wooll of Bat, and Tongue of Dogge:
Adders Forke, and Blinde-wormes Sting,
Lizards legge, and Howlets wing:
For a Charme of powrefull trouble,
Like a Hell-broth, boyle and bubble

   All. Double, double, toyle and trouble,
Fire burne, and Cauldron bubble

   3 Scale of Dragon, Tooth of Wolfe,
Witches Mummey, Maw, and Gulfe
Of the rauin'd salt Sea sharke:
Roote of Hemlocke, digg'd i'th' darke:
Liuer of Blaspheming Iew,
Gall of Goate, and Slippes of Yew,
Sliuer'd in the Moones Ecclipse:
Nose of Turke, and Tartars lips:
Finger of Birth-strangled Babe,
Ditch-deliuer'd by a Drab,
Make the Grewell thicke, and slab.
Adde thereto a Tigers Chawdron,
For th' Ingredience of our Cawdron

   All. Double, double, toyle and trouble,
Fire burne, and Cauldron bubble

2 Coole it with a Baboones blood, Then the Charme is firme and good.
Enter Hecat, and the other three Witches.

   Hec. O well done: I commend your paines,
And euery one shall share i'th' gaines:
And now about the Cauldron sing
Like Elues and Fairies in a Ring,
Inchanting all that you put in.

Musicke and a Song. Blacke Spirits, &c.

  2 By the pricking of my Thumbes,
Something wicked this way comes:
Open Lockes, who euer knockes.
Enter Macbeth.

  Macb. How now you secret, black, & midnight Hags?
What is't you do?
  All. A deed without a name

  Macb. I coniure you, by that which you Professe,
(How ere you come to know it) answer me:
Though you vntye the Windes, and let them fight
Against the Churches: Though the yesty Waues
Confound and swallow Nauigation vp:
Though bladed Corne be lodg'd, & Trees blown downe,
Though Castles topple on their Warders heads:
Though Pallaces, and Pyramids do slope
Their heads to their Foundations: Though the treasure
Of Natures Germaine, tumble altogether,
Euen till destruction sicken: Answer me
To what I aske you

1 Speake

2 Demand

3 Wee'l answer

        1 Say, if th'hadst rather heare it from our mouthes, Or
        from our Masters

Macb. Call 'em: let me see 'em

  1 Powre in Sowes blood, that hath eaten
Her nine Farrow: Greaze that's sweaten
From the Murderers Gibbet, throw
Into the Flame

All. Come high or low:
Thy Selfe and Office deaftly show.
Thunder. 1. Apparation, an Armed Head.

Macb. Tell me, thou vnknowne power

     1 He knowes thy thought: Heare his speech, but say thou
     nought

1 Appar. Macbeth, Macbeth, Macbeth: Beware Macduffe, Beware the
Thane of Fife: dismisse me. Enough.

He Descends.

  Macb. What ere thou art, for thy good caution, thanks
Thou hast harp'd my feare aright. But one word more

   1 He will not be commanded: heere's another
More potent then the first.

Thunder. 2 Apparition, a Bloody Childe.

2 Appar. Macbeth, Macbeth, Macbeth

Macb. Had I three eares, Il'd heare thee

  Appar. Be bloody, bold, & resolute:
Laugh to scorne
The powre of man: For none of woman borne
Shall harme Macbeth.

Descends.

  Mac. Then liue Macduffe: what need I feare of thee?
But yet Ile make assurance: double sure,
And take a Bond of Fate: thou shalt not liue,
That I may tell pale-hearted Feare, it lies;
And sleepe in spight of Thunder.

Thunder 3 Apparation, a Childe Crowned, with a Tree in his hand.

What is this, that rises like the issue of a King,
And weares vpon his Baby-brow, the round

And top of Soueraignty?
  All. Listen, but speake not too't

  3 Appar. Be Lyon metled, proud, and take no care:
Who chafes, who frets, or where Conspirers are:
Macbeth shall neuer vanquish'd be, vntill
Great Byrnam Wood, to high Dunsmane Hill
Shall come against him.

Descend.

  Macb. That will neuer bee:
Who can impresse the Forrest, bid the Tree
Vnfixe his earth-bound Root? Sweet boadments, good:
Rebellious dead, rise neuer till the Wood
Of Byrnan rise, and our high plac'd Macbeth
Shall liue the Lease of Nature, pay his breath
To time, and mortall Custome. Yet my Hart
Throbs to know one thing: Tell me, if your Art
Can tell so much: Shall Banquo's issue euer
Reigne in this Kingdome?
  All. Seeke to know no more

  Macb. I will be satisfied. Deny me this,
And an eternall Curse fall on you: Let me know.
Why sinkes that Caldron? & what noise is this?

Hoboyes

1 Shew

2 Shew

3 Shew

  All. Shew his Eyes, and greeue his Hart,
Come like shadowes, so depart.

A shew of eight Kings, and Banquo last, with a glasse in his hand.

  Macb. Thou art too like the Spirit of Banquo: Down:
Thy Crowne do's seare mine Eye-bals. And thy haire

Thou other Gold-bound-brow, is like the first:
A third, is like the former. Filthy Hagges,
Why do you shew me this? - A fourth? Start eyes!
What will the Line stretch out to'th' cracke of Doome?
Another yet? A seauenth? Ile see no more:
And yet the eighth appeares, who beares a glasse,
Which shewes me many more: and some I see,
That two-fold Balles, and trebble Scepters carry.
Horrible sight: Now I see 'tis true,
For the Blood-bolter'd Banquo smiles vpon me,
And points at them for his. What? is this so?
  1 I Sir, all this is so. But why
Stands Macbeth thus amazedly?
Come Sisters, cheere we vp his sprights,
And shew the best of our delights.
Ile Charme the Ayre to giue a sound,
While you performe your Antique round:
That this great King may kindly say,
Our duties, did his welcome pay.

Musicke. The Witches Dance, and vanish.

  Macb. Where are they? Gone?
Let this pernitious houre,
Stand aye accursed in the Kalender.
Come in, without there.
Enter Lenox.

Lenox. What's your Graces will

  Macb. Saw you the Weyard Sisters?
Lenox. No my Lord

  Macb. Came they not by you?
Lenox. No indeed my Lord

  Macb. Infected be the Ayre whereon they ride,
And damn'd all those that trust them. I did heare
The gallopping of Horse. Who was't came by?

Len. 'Tis two or three my Lord, that bring you word:
Macduff is fled to England

  Macb. Fled to England?
  Len. I, my good Lord

  Macb. Time, thou anticipat'st my dread exploits:
The flighty purpose neuer is o're-tooke
Vnlesse the deed go with it. From this moment,
The very firstlings of my heart shall be
The firstlings of my hand. And euen now
To Crown my thoughts with Acts: be it thoght & done:
The Castle of Macduff, I will surprize.
Seize vpon Fife; giue to th' edge o'th' Sword
His Wife, his Babes, and all vnfortunate Soules
That trace him in his Line. No boasting like a Foole,
This deed Ile do, before this purpose coole,
But no more sights. Where are these Gentlemen?
Come bring me where they are.

Exeunt.

Scena Secunda.

Enter Macduffes Wife, her Son, and Rosse.

  Wife. What had he done, to make him fly the Land?
  Rosse. You must haue patience Madam

  Wife. He had none:
His flight was madnesse: when our Actions do not,
Our feares do make vs Traitors

  Rosse. You know not
Whether it was his wisedome, or his feare

  Wife. Wisedom? to leaue his wife, to leaue his Babes,
His Mansion, and his Titles, in a place
From whence himselfe do's flye? He loues vs not,
He wants the naturall touch. For the poore Wren
(The most diminitiue of Birds) will fight,

Her yong ones in her Nest, against the Owle:
All is the Feare, and nothing is the Loue;
As little is the Wisedome, where the flight
So runnes against all reason

   Rosse. My deerest Cooz,
I pray you schoole your selfe. But for your Husband,
He is Noble, Wise, Iudicious, and best knowes
The fits o'th' Season. I dare not speake much further,
But cruell are the times, when we are Traitors
And do not know our selues: when we hold Rumor
From what we feare, yet know not what we feare,
But floate vpon a wilde and violent Sea
Each way, and moue. I take my leaue of you:
Shall not be long but Ile be heere againe:
Things at the worst will cease, or else climbe vpward,
To what they were before. My pretty Cosine,
Blessing vpon you

   Wife. Father'd he is,
And yet hee's Father-lesse

   Rosse. I am so much a Foole, should I stay longer
It would be my disgrace, and your discomfort.
I take my leaue at once.

Exit Rosse.

  Wife. Sirra, your Fathers dead,
And what will you do now? How will you liue?
  Son. As Birds do Mother

  Wife. What with Wormes, and Flyes?
  Son. With what I get I meane, and so do they

  Wife. Poore Bird,
Thou'dst neuer Feare the Net, nor Lime,
The Pitfall, nor the Gin

Son. Why should I Mother?
Poore Birds they are not set for:
My Father is not dead for all your saying

Wife. Yes, he is dead:
How wilt thou do for a Father?
  Son. Nay how will you do for a Husband?
  Wife. Why I can buy me twenty at any Market

Son. Then you'l by 'em to sell againe

Wife. Thou speak'st withall thy wit,
And yet I'faith with wit enough for thee

  Son. Was my Father a Traitor, Mother?
  Wife. I, that he was

  Son. What is a Traitor?
  Wife. Why one that sweares, and lyes

Son. And be all Traitors, that do so

  Wife. Euery one that do's so, is a Traitor,
And must be hang'd

  Son. And must they all be hang'd, that swear and lye?
  Wife. Euery one

  Son. Who must hang them?
  Wife. Why, the honest men

Son. Then the Liars and Swearers are Fools: for there are Lyars and
Swearers enow, to beate the honest men, and hang vp them

Wife. Now God helpe thee, poore Monkie: But how wilt thou do for a
Father? Son. If he were dead, youl'd weepe for him: if you would not, it
were a good signe, that I should quickely haue a new Father

  Wife. Poore pratler, how thou talk'st?
Enter a Messenger.

  Mes. Blesse you faire Dame: I am not to you known,
Though in your state of Honor I am perfect;

I doubt some danger do's approach you neerely.
If you will take a homely mans aduice,
Be not found heere: Hence with your little ones
To fright you thus. Me thinkes I am too sauage:
To do worse to you, were fell Cruelty,
Which is too nie your person. Heauen preserue you,
I dare abide no longer.

Exit Messenger

  Wife. Whether should I flye?
I haue done no harme. But I remember now
I am in this earthly world: where to do harme
Is often laudable, to do good sometime
Accounted dangerous folly. Why then (alas)
Do I put vp that womanly defence,
To say I haue done no harme?
What are these faces?
Enter Murtherers.

  Mur. Where is your Husband?
  Wife. I hope in no place so vnsanctified,
Where such as thou may'st finde him

Mur. He's a Traitor

Son. Thou ly'st thou shagge-ear'd Villaine

  Mur. What you Egge?
Yong fry of Treachery?
  Son. He ha's kill'd me Mother,
Run away I pray you.

Exit crying Murther.

Scaena Tertia.

Enter Malcolme and Macduffe.

  Mal. Let vs seeke out some desolate shade, & there
Weepe our sad bosomes empty

Macd. Let vs rather
Hold fast the mortall Sword: and like good men,
Bestride our downfall Birthdome: each new Morne,
New Widdowes howle, new Orphans cry, new sorowes
Strike heauen on the face, that it resounds
As if it felt with Scotland, and yell'd out
Like Syllable of Dolour

Mal. What I beleeue, Ile waile;
What know, beleeue; and what I can redresse,
As I shall finde the time to friend: I wil.
What you haue spoke, it may be so perchance.
This Tyrant, whose sole name blisters our tongues,
Was once thought honest: you haue lou'd him well,
He hath not touch'd you yet. I am yong, but something
You may discerne of him through me, and wisedome
To offer vp a weake, poore innocent Lambe
T' appease an angry God

Macd. I am not treacherous

Malc. But Macbeth is.
A good and vertuous Nature may recoyle
In an Imperiall charge. But I shall craue your pardon:
That which you are, my thoughts cannot transpose;
Angels are bright still, though the brightest fell.
Though all things foule, would wear the brows of grace
Yet Grace must still looke so

Macd. I haue lost my Hopes

Malc. Perchance euen there
Where I did finde my doubts.
Why in that rawnesse left you Wife, and Childe?
Those precious Motiues, those strong knots of Loue,
Without leaue-taking. I pray you,
Let not my Iealousies, be your Dishonors,
But mine owne Safeties: you may be rightly iust,
What euer I shall thinke

Macd. Bleed, bleed poore Country,
Great Tyrrany, lay thou thy basis sure,
For goodnesse dare not check thee: wear y thy wrongs,
The Title, is affear'd. Far thee well Lord,
I would not be the Villaine that thou think'st,
For the whole Space that's in the Tyrants Graspe,
And the rich East to boot

Mal. Be not offended:
I speake not as in absolute feare of you:
I thinke our Country sinkes beneath the yoake,
It weepes, it bleeds, and each new day a gash
Is added to her wounds. I thinke withall,
There would be hands vplifted in my right:
And heere from gracious England haue I offer
Of goodly thousands. But for all this,
When I shall treade vpon the Tyrants head,
Or weare it on my Sword; yet my poore Country
Shall haue more vices then it had before,
More suffer, and more sundry wayes then euer,
By him that shall succeede

Macd. What should he be?
Mal. It is my selfe I meane: in whom I know
All the particulars of Vice so grafted,
That when they shall be open'd, blacke Macbeth
Will seeme as pure as Snow, and the poore State
Esteeme him as a Lambe, being compar'd
With my confinelesse harmes

Macd. Not in the Legions
Of horrid Hell, can come a Diuell more damn'd
In euils, to top Macbeth

Mal. I grant him Bloody,
Luxurious, Auaricious, False, Deceitfull,
Sodaine, Malicious, smacking of euery sinne
That ha's a name. But there's no bottome, none
In my Voluptuousnesse: Your Wiues, your Daughters,
Your Matrons, and your Maides, could not fill vp

The Cesterne of my Lust, and my Desire
All continent Impediments would ore-beare
That did oppose my will. Better Macbeth,
Then such an one to reigne

    Macd. Boundlesse intemperance
In Nature is a Tyranny: It hath beene
Th' vntimely emptying of the happy Throne,
And fall of many Kings. But feare not yet
To take vpon you what is yours: you may
Conuey your pleasures in a spacious plenty,
And yet seeme cold. The time you may so hoodwinke:
We haue willing Dames enough: there cannot be
That Vulture in you, to deuoure so many
As will to Greatnesse dedicate themselues,
Finding it so inclinde

    Mal. With this, there growes
In my most ill-composd Affection, such
A stanchlesse Auarice, that were I King,
I should cut off the Nobles for their Lands,
Desire his Iewels, and this others House,
And my more-hauing, would be as a Sawce
To make me hunger more, that I should forge
Quarrels vniust against the Good and Loyall,
Destroying them for wealth

    Macd. This Auarice
stickes deeper: growes with more pernicious roote
Then Summer-seeming Lust: and it hath bin
The Sword of our slaine Kings: yet do not feare,
Scotland hath Foysons, to fill vp your will
Of your meere Owne. All these are portable,
With other Graces weigh'd

    Mal. But I haue none. The King-becoming Graces,
As Iustice, Verity, Temp'rance, Stablenesse,
Bounty, Perseuerance, Mercy, Lowlinesse,
Deuotion, Patience, Courage, Fortitude,
I haue no rellish of them, but abound

In the diuision of each seuerall Crime,
Acting it many wayes. Nay, had I powre, I should
Poure the sweet Milke of Concord, into Hell,
Vprore the vniuersall peace, confound
All vnity on earth

Macd. O Scotland, Scotland

  Mal. If such a one be fit to gouerne, speake:
I am as I haue spoken

  Mac. Fit to gouern? No not to liue. O Natio[n] miserable!
With an vntitled Tyrant, bloody Sceptred,
When shalt thou see thy wholsome dayes againe?
Since that the truest Issue of thy Throne
By his owne Interdiction stands accust,
And do's blaspheme his breed? Thy Royall Father
Was a most Sainted-King: the Queene that bore thee,
Oftner vpon her knees, then on her feet,
Dy'de euery day she liu'd. Fare thee well,
These Euils thou repeat'st vpon thy selfe,
Hath banish'd me from Scotland. O my Brest,
Thy hope ends heere

  Mal. Macduff, this Noble passion
Childe of integrity, hath from my soule
Wip'd the blacke Scruples, reconcil'd my thoughts
To thy good Truth, and Honor. Diuellish Macbeth,
By many of these traines, hath sought to win me
Into his power: and modest Wisedome pluckes me
From ouer-credulous hast: but God aboue
Deale betweene thee and me; For euen now
I put my selfe to thy Direction, and
Vnspeake mine owne detraction. Heere abiure
The taints, and blames I laide vpon my selfe,
For strangers to my Nature. I am yet
Vnknowne to Woman, neuer was forsworne,
Scarsely haue coueted what was mine owne.
At no time broke my Faith, would not betray
The Deuill to his Fellow, and delight

No lesse in truth then life. My first false speaking
Was this vpon my selfe. What I am truly
Is thine, and my poore Countries to command:
Whither indeed, before they heere approach
Old Seyward with ten thousand warlike men
Already at a point, was setting foorth:
Now wee'l together, and the chance of goodnesse
Be like our warranted Quarrell. Why are you silent?
  Macd. Such welcome, and vnwelcom things at once
'Tis hard to reconcile.
Enter a Doctor.

  Mal. Well, more anon. Comes the King forth
I pray you?
  Doct. I Sir: there are a crew of wretched Soules
That stay his Cure: their malady conuinces
The great assay of Art. But at his touch,
Such sanctity hath Heauen giuen his hand,
They presently amend.
Enter.

Mal. I thanke you Doctor

  Macd. What's the Disease he meanes?
  Mal. Tis call'd the Euill.
A most myraculous worke in this good King,
Which often since my heere remaine in England,
I haue seene him do: How he solicites heauen
Himselfe best knowes: but strangely visited people
All swolne and Vlcerous, pittifull to the eye,
The meere dispaire of Surgery, he cures,
Hanging a golden stampe about their neckes,
Put on with holy Prayers, and 'tis spoken
To the succeeding Royalty he leaues
The healing Benediction. With this strange vertue,
He hath a heauenly guift of Prophesie,
And sundry Blessings hang about his Throne,
That speake him full of Grace.
Enter Rosse.

Macd. See who comes heere

Malc. My Countryman: but yet I know him not

Macd. My euer gentle Cozen, welcome hither

   Malc. I know him now. Good God betimes remoue
The meanes that makes vs Strangers

Rosse. Sir, Amen

   Macd. Stands Scotland where it did?
   Rosse. Alas poore Countrey,
Almost affraid to know it selfe. It cannot
Be call'd our Mother, but our Graue; where nothing
But who knowes nothing, is once seene to smile:
Where sighes, and groanes, and shrieks that rent the ayre
Are made, not mark'd: Where violent sorrow seemes
A Moderne extasie: The Deadmans knell,
Is there scarse ask'd for who, and good mens liues
Expire before the Flowers in their Caps,
Dying, or ere they sicken

Macd. Oh Relation; too nice, and yet too true

   Malc. What's the newest griefe?
   Rosse. That of an houres age, doth hisse the speaker,
Each minute teemes a new one

   Macd. How do's my Wife?
   Rosse. Why well

   Macd. And all my Children?
   Rosse. Well too

   Macd. The Tyrant ha's not batter'd at their peace?
   Rosse. No, they were wel at peace, when I did leaue 'em
   Macd. Be not a niggard of your speech: How gos't?
   Rosse. When I came hither to transport the Tydings
Which I haue heauily borne, there ran a Rumour
Of many worthy Fellowes, that were out,
Which was to my beleefe witnest the rather,

For that I saw the Tyrants Power a-foot.
Now is the time of helpe: your eye in Scotland
Would create Soldiours, make our women fight,
To doffe their dire distresses

  Malc. Bee't their comfort
We are comming thither: Gracious England hath
Lent vs good Seyward, and ten thousand men,
An older, and a better Souldier, none
That Christendome giues out

  Rosse. Would I could answer
This comfort with the like. But I haue words
That would be howl'd out in the desert ayre,
Where hearing should not latch them

  Macd. What concerne they,
The generall cause, or is it a Fee-griefe
Due to some single brest?
  Rosse. No minde that's honest
But in it shares some woe, though the maine part
Pertaines to you alone

  Macd. If it be mine
Keepe it not from me, quickly let me haue it

Rosse. Let not your eares dispise my tongue for euer, Which shall
possesse them with the heauiest sound that euer yet they heard

Macd. Humh: I guesse at it

  Rosse. Your Castle is surpriz'd: your Wife, and Babes
Sauagely slaughter'd: To relate the manner
Were on the Quarry of these murther'd Deere
To adde the death of you

  Malc. Mercifull Heauen:
What man, ne're pull your hat vpon your browes:
Giue sorrow words; the griefe that do's not speake,
Whispers the o're-fraught heart, and bids it breake

Macd. My Children too?

Ro. Wife, Children, Seruants, all that could be found

Macd. And I must be from thence? My wife kil'd too?

Rosse. I haue said

Malc. Be comforted.
Let's make vs Med'cines of our great Reuenge,
To cure this deadly greefe

Macd. He ha's no Children. All my pretty ones?
Did you say All? Oh Hell-Kite! All?
What, All my pretty Chickens, and their Damme
At one fell swoope?

Malc. Dispute it like a man

Macd. I shall do so:
But I must also feele it as a man;
I cannot but remember such things were
That were most precious to me: Did heauen looke on,
And would not take their part? Sinfull Macduff,
They were all strooke for thee: Naught that I am,
Not for their owne demerits, but for mine
Fell slaughter on their soules: Heauen rest them now

Mal. Be this the Whetstone of your sword, let griefe
Conuert to anger: blunt not the heart, enrage it

Macd. O I could play the woman with mine eyes,
And Braggart with my tongue. But gentle Heauens,
Cut short all intermission: Front to Front,
Bring thou this Fiend of Scotland, and my selfe
Within my Swords length set him, if he scape
Heauen forgiue him too

Mal. This time goes manly:
Come go we to the King, our Power is ready,
Our lacke is nothing but our leaue. Macbeth
Is ripe for shaking, and the Powres aboue
Put on their Instruments: Receiue what cheere you may,
The Night is long, that neuer findes the Day.

Exeunt.

Actus Quintus. Scena Prima.

Enter a Doctor of Physicke, and a Wayting Gentlewoman.

Doct. I haue too Nights watch'd with you, but can perceiue no truth in your report. When was it shee last walk'd? Gent. Since his Maiesty went into the Field, I haue seene her rise from her bed, throw her Night-Gown vppon her, vnlocke her Closset, take foorth paper, folde it, write vpon't, read it, afterwards Seale it, and againe returne to bed; yet all this while in a most fast sleepe

Doct. A great perturbation in Nature, to receyue at once the benefit of sleep, and do the effects of watching. In this slumbry agitation, besides her walking, and other actuall performances, what (at any time) haue you heard her say? Gent. That Sir, which I will not report after her

Doct. You may to me, and 'tis most meet you should

Gent. Neither to you, nor any one, hauing no witnesse to confirme my speech. Enter Lady, with a Taper.

Lo you, heere she comes: This is her very guise, and vpon my life fast asleepe: obserue her, stand close

  Doct. How came she by that light?
  Gent. Why it stood by her: she ha's light by her continually,
'tis her command

Doct. You see her eyes are open

Gent. I, but their sense are shut

  Doct. What is it she do's now?
Looke how she rubbes her hands

Gent. It is an accustom'd action with her, to seeme thus washing her hands: I haue knowne her continue in this a quarter of an houre

Lad. Yet heere's a spot

Doct. Heark, she speaks, I will set downe what comes
from her, to satisfie my remembrance the more strongly

La. Out damned spot: out I say. One: Two: Why then 'tis time to doo't:
Hell is murky. Fye, my Lord, fie, a Souldier, and affear'd? what need
we feare? who knowes it, when none can call our powre to accompt:
yet who would haue thought the olde man to haue had so much blood
in him

Doct. Do you marke that?
Lad. The Thane of Fife, had a wife: where is she now?
What will these hands ne're be cleane? No more o'that
my Lord, no more o'that: you marre all with this starting

Doct. Go too, go too:
You haue knowne what you should not

Gent. She ha's spoke what shee should not, I am sure
of that: Heauen knowes what she ha's knowne

La. Heere's the smell of the blood still: all the perfumes of Arabia will
not sweeten this little hand. Oh, oh, oh

Doct. What a sigh is there? The hart is sorely charg'd

Gent. I would not haue such a heart in my bosome, for
the dignity of the whole body

Doct. Well, well, well

Gent. Pray God it be sir

Doct. This disease is beyond my practise: yet I haue knowne those
which haue walkt in their sleep, who haue dyed holily in their beds

Lad. Wash your hands, put on your Night-Gowne, looke not so pale: I
tell you yet againe Banquo's buried; he cannot come out on's graue

Doct. Euen so?
Lady. To bed, to bed: there's knocking at the gate:
Come, come, come, come, giue me your hand: What's
done, cannot be vndone. To bed, to bed, to bed.

Exit Lady.

Doct. Will she go now to bed?
Gent. Directly

Doct. Foule whisp'rings are abroad: vnnaturall deeds
Do breed vnnaturall troubles: infected mindes
To their deafe pillowes will discharge their Secrets:
More needs she the Diuine, then the Physitian:
God, God forgiue vs all. Looke after her,
Remoue from her the meanes of all annoyance,
And still keepe eyes vpon her: So goodnight,
My minde she ha's mated, and amaz'd my sight.
I thinke, but dare not speake

Gent. Good night good Doctor.

Exeunt.

Scena Secunda.

Drum and Colours. Enter Menteth, Cathnes, Angus, Lenox,
Soldiers.

Ment. The English powre is neere, led on by Malcolm,
His Vnkle Seyward, and the good Macduff.
Reuenges burne in them: for their deere causes
Would to the bleeding, and the grim Alarme
Excite the mortified man

Ang. Neere Byrnan wood
Shall we well meet them, that way are they comming

Cath. Who knowes if Donalbane be with his brother?
Len. For certaine Sir, he is not: I haue a File
Of all the Gentry; there is Seywards Sonne,
And many vnruffe youths, that euen now
Protest their first of Manhood

Ment. What do's the Tyrant

Cath. Great Dunsinane he strongly Fortifies:
Some say hee's mad: Others, that lesser hate him,
Do call it valiant Fury, but for certaine
He cannot buckle his distemper'd cause
Within the belt of Rule

Ang. Now do's he feele
His secret Murthers sticking on his hands,
Now minutely Reuolts vpbraid his Faith-breach:
Those he commands, moue onely in command,
Nothing in loue: Now do's he feele his Title
Hang loose about him, like a Giants Robe
Vpon a dwarfish Theefe

Ment. Who then shall blame
His pester'd Senses to recoyle, and start,
When all that is within him, do's condemne
It selfe, for being there

Cath. Well, march we on,
To giue Obedience, where 'tis truly ow'd:
Meet we the Med'cine of the sickly Weale,
And with him poure we in our Countries purge,
Each drop of vs

Lenox. Or so much as it needes,
To dew the Soueraigne Flower, and drowne the Weeds:
Make we our March towards Birnan.

Exeunt. marching.

Scaena Tertia.

Enter Macbeth, Doctor, and Attendants.

Macb. Bring me no more Reports, let them flye all:
Till Byrnane wood remoue to Dunsinane,
I cannot taint with Feare. What's the Boy Malcolme?
Was he not borne of woman? The Spirits that know
All mortall Consequences, haue pronounc'd me thus:

Feare not Macbeth, no man that's borne of woman
Shall ere haue power vpon thee. Then fly false Thanes,
And mingle with the English Epicures,
The minde I sway by, and the heart I beare,
Shall neuer sagge with doubt, nor shake with feare.
Enter Seruant.

The diuell damne thee blacke, thou cream-fac'd Loone:
Where got'st thou that Goose-looke

Ser. There is ten thousand

   Macb. Geese Villaine?
   Ser. Souldiers Sir

   Macb. Go pricke thy face, and ouer-red thy feare
Thou Lilly-liuer'd Boy. What Soldiers, Patch?
Death of thy Soule, those Linnen cheekes of thine
Are Counsailers to feare. What Soldiers Whay-face?
   Ser. The English Force, so please you

   Macb. Take thy face hence. Seyton, I am sick at hart,
When I behold: Seyton, I say, this push
Will cheere me euer, or dis-eate me now.
I haue liu'd long enough: my way of life
Is falne into the Seare, the yellow Leafe,
And that which should accompany Old-Age,
As Honor, Loue, Obedience, Troopes of Friends,
I must not looke to haue: but in their steed,
Curses, not lowd but deepe, Mouth-honor, breath
Which the poore heart would faine deny, and dare not.
Seyton?
Enter Seyton.

   Sey. What's your gracious pleasure?
   Macb. What Newes more?
   Sey. All is confirm'd my Lord, which was reported

   Macb. Ile fight, till from my bones, my flesh be hackt.
Giue me my Armor

Seyt. 'Tis not needed yet

  Macb. Ile put it on:
Send out moe Horses, skirre the Country round,
Hang those that talke of Feare. Giue me mine Armor:
How do's your Patient, Doctor?
  Doct. Not so sicke my Lord,
As she is troubled with thicke-comming Fancies
That keepe her from her rest

  Macb. Cure of that:
Can'st thou not Minister to a minde diseas'd,
Plucke from the Memory a rooted Sorrow,
Raze out the written troubles of the Braine,
And with some sweet Obliuious Antidote
Cleanse the stufft bosome, of that perillous stuffe
Which weighes vpon the heart?
  Doct. Therein the Patient
Must minister to himselfe

  Macb. Throw Physicke to the Dogs, Ile none of it.
Come, put mine Armour on: giue me my Staffe:
Seyton, send out: Doctor, the Thanes flye from me:
Come sir, dispatch. If thou could'st Doctor, cast
The Water of my Land, finde her Disease,
And purge it to a sound and pristine Health,
I would applaud thee to the very Eccho,
That should applaud againe. Pull't off I say,
What Rubarb, Cyme, or what Purgatiue drugge
Would scowre these English hence: hear'st y of them?
  Doct. I my good Lord: your Royall Preparation
Makes vs heare something

  Macb. Bring it after me:
I will not be affraid of Death and Bane,
Till Birnane Forrest come to Dunsinane

  Doct. Were I from Dunsinane away, and cleere,
Profit againe should hardly draw me heere.

Exeunt.

Scena Quarta.

Drum and Colours. Enter Malcolme, Seyward, Macduffe,
Seywards Sonne,
Menteth, Cathnes, Angus, and Soldiers Marching.

  Malc. Cosins, I hope the dayes are neere at hand
That Chambers will be safe

Ment. We doubt it nothing

  Seyw. What wood is this before vs?
  Ment. The wood of Birnane

  Malc. Let euery Souldier hew him downe a Bough,
And bear't before him, thereby shall we shadow
The numbers of our Hoast, and make discouery
Erre in report of vs

Sold. It shall be done

  Syw. We learne no other, but the confident Tyrant
Keepes still in Dunsinane, and will indure
Our setting downe befor't

  Malc. 'Tis his maine hope:
For where there is aduantage to be giuen,
Both more and lesse haue giuen him the Reuolt,
And none serue with him, but constrained things,
Whose hearts are absent too

  Macd. Let our iust Censures
Attend the true euent, and put we on
Industrious Souldiership

  Sey. The time approaches,
That will with due decision make vs know
What we shall say we haue, and what we owe:
Thoughts speculatiue, their vnsure hopes relate,

But certaine issue, stroakes must arbitrate,
Towards which, aduance the warre.

Exeunt. marching

Scena Quinta.

Enter Macbeth, Seyton, & Souldiers, with Drum and Colours.

Macb. Hang out our Banners on the outward walls,
The Cry is still, they come: our Castles strength
Will laugh a Siedge to scorne: Heere let them lye,
Till Famine and the Ague eate them vp:
Were they not forc'd with those that should be ours,
We might haue met them darefull, beard to beard,
And beate them backward home. What is that noyse?

A Cry within of Women.

Sey. It is the cry of women, my good Lord

Macb. I haue almost forgot the taste of Feares:
The time ha's beene, my sences would haue cool'd
To heare a Night-shrieke, and my Fell of haire
Would at a dismall Treatise rowze, and stirre
As life were in't. I haue supt full with horrors,
Direnesse familiar to my slaughterous thoughts
Cannot once start me. Wherefore was that cry?
Sey. The Queene (my Lord) is dead

Macb. She should haue dy'de heereafter;
There would haue beene a time for such a word:
To morrow, and to morrow, and to morrow,
Creepes in this petty pace from day to day,
To the last Syllable of Recorded time:
And all our yesterdayes, haue lighted Fooles
The way to dusty death. Out, out, breefe Candle,
Life's but a walking Shadow, a poore Player,
That struts and frets his houre vpon the Stage,
And then is heard no more. It is a Tale
Told by an Ideot, full of sound and fury

Signifying nothing.
Enter a Messenger.

Thou com'st to vse thy Tongue: thy Story quickly

  Mes. Gracious my Lord,
I should report that which I say I saw,
But know not how to doo't

Macb. Well, say sir

  Mes. As I did stand my watch vpon the Hill
I look'd toward Byrnane, and anon me thought
The Wood began to moue

Macb. Lyar, and Slaue

  Mes. Let me endure your wrath, if't be not so:
Within this three Mile may you see it comming.
I say, a mouing Groue

  Macb. If thou speak'st false,
Vpon the next Tree shall thou hang aliue
Till Famine cling thee: If thy speech be sooth,
I care not if thou dost for me as much.
I pull in Resolution, and begin
To doubt th' Equiuocation of the Fiend,
That lies like truth. Feare not, till Byrnane Wood
Do come to Dunsinane, and now a Wood
Comes toward Dunsinane. Arme, Arme, and out,
If this which he auouches, do's appeare,
There is nor flying hence, nor tarrying here.
I 'ginne to be a-weary of the Sun,
And wish th' estate o'th' world were now vndon.
Ring the Alarum Bell, blow Winde, come wracke,
At least wee'l dye with Harnesse on our backe.

Exeunt.

Scena Sexta.

Drumme and Colours. Enter Malcolme, Seyward, Macduffe, and their Army, with Boughes.

  Mal. Now neere enough:
Your leauy Skreenes throw downe,
And shew like those you are: You (worthy Vnkle)
Shall with my Cosin your right Noble Sonne
Leade our first Battell. Worthy Macduffe, and wee
Shall take vpon's what else remaines to do,
According to our order

  Sey. Fare you well:
Do we but finde the Tyrants power to night,
Let vs be beaten, if we cannot fight

  Macd. Make all our Trumpets speak, giue the[m] all breath
Those clamorous Harbingers of Blood, & Death.

Exeunt.

Alarums continued.

Scena Septima.

Enter Macbeth.

  Macb. They haue tied me to a stake, I cannot flye,
But Beare-like I must fight the course. What's he
That was not borne of Woman? Such a one
Am I to feare, or none.
Enter young Seyward.

  Y.Sey. What is thy name?
Macb. Thou'lt be affraid to heare it

  Y.Sey. No: though thou call'st thy selfe a hoter name
Then any is in hell

Macb. My name's Macbeth

Y.Sey. The diuell himselfe could not pronounce a Title
More hatefull to mine eare

Macb. No: nor more fearefull

Y.Sey. Thou lyest abhorred Tyrant, with my Sword
Ile proue the lye thou speak'st.

Fight, and young Seyward slaine.

Macb. Thou was't borne of woman;
But Swords I smile at, Weapons laugh to scorne,
Brandish'd by man that's of a Woman borne.
Enter.

Alarums. Enter Macduffe.

Macd. That way the noise is: Tyrant shew thy face,
If thou beest slaine, and with no stroake of mine,
My Wife and Childrens Ghosts will haunt me still:
I cannot strike at wretched Kernes, whose armes
Are hyr'd to beare their Staues; either thou Macbeth,
Or else my Sword with an vnbattered edge
I sheath againe vndeeded. There thou should'st be,
By this great clatter, one of greatest note
Seemes bruited. Let me finde him Fortune,
And more I begge not.

Exit. Alarums.

Enter Malcolme and Seyward.

Sey. This way my Lord, the Castles gently rendred:
The Tyrants people, on both sides do fight,
The Noble Thanes do brauely in the Warre,
The day almost it selfe professes yours,
And little is to do

Malc. We haue met with Foes
That strike beside vs

Sey. Enter Sir, the Castle.

Exeunt. Alarum

Enter Macbeth.

  Macb. Why should I play the Roman Foole, and dye
On mine owne sword? whiles I see liues, the gashes
Do better vpon them.
Enter Macduffe.

Macd. Turne Hell-hound, turne

  Macb. Of all men else I haue auoyded thee:
But get thee backe, my soule is too much charg'd
With blood of thine already

  Macd. I haue no words,
My voice is in my Sword, thou bloodier Villaine
Then tearmes can giue thee out.

Fight: Alarum

  Macb. Thou loosest labour
As easie may'st thou the intrenchant Ayre
With thy keene Sword impresse, as make me bleed:
Let fall thy blade on vulnerable Crests,
I beare a charmed Life, which must not yeeld
To one of woman borne

  Macd. Dispaire thy Charme,
And let the Angell whom thou still hast seru'd
Tell thee, Macduffe was from his Mothers womb
Vntimely ript

  Macb. Accursed be that tongue that tels mee so;
For it hath Cow'd my better part of man:
And be these Iugling Fiends no more beleeu'd,
That palter with vs in a double sence,
That keepe the word of promise to our eare,
And breake it to our hope. Ile not fight with thee

  Macd. Then yeeld thee Coward,
And liue to be the shew, and gaze o'th' time.

Wee'l haue thee, as our rarer Monsters are
Painted vpon a pole, and vnder-writ,
Heere may you see the Tyrant

  Macb. I will not yeeld
To kisse the ground before young Malcolmes feet,
And to be baited with the Rabbles curse.
Though Byrnane wood be come to Dunsinane,
And thou oppos'd, being of no woman borne,
Yet I will try the last. Before my body,
I throw my warlike Shield: Lay on Macduffe,
And damn'd be him, that first cries hold, enough.

Exeunt. fighting. Alarums.

Enter Fighting, and Macbeth slaine.

Retreat, and Flourish. Enter with Drumme and Colours, Malcolm,
Seyward,
Rosse, Thanes, & Soldiers.

Mal. I would the Friends we misse, were safe arriu'd

  Sey. Some must go off: and yet by these I see,
So great a day as this is cheapely bought

Mal. Macduffe is missing, and your Noble Sonne

  Rosse. Your son my Lord, ha's paid a souldiers debt,
He onely liu'd but till he was a man,
The which no sooner had his Prowesse confirm'd
In the vnshrinking station where he fought,
But like a man he dy'de

  Sey. Then he is dead?
  Rosse. I, and brought off the field: your cause of sorrow
Must not be measur'd by his worth, for then
It hath no end

  Sey. Had he his hurts before?
  Rosse. I, on the Front

Sey. Why then, Gods Soldier be he:
Had I as many Sonnes, as I haue haires,
I would not wish them to a fairer death:
And so his Knell is knoll'd

  Mal. Hee's worth more sorrow,
and that Ile spend for him

  Sey. He's worth no more,
They say he parted well, and paid his score,
And so God be with him. Here comes newer comfort.
Enter Macduffe, with Macbeths head.

  Macd. Haile King, for so thou art.
Behold where stands
Th' Vsurpers cursed head: the time is free:
I see thee compast with thy Kingdomes Pearle,
That speake my salutation in their minds:
Whose voyces I desire alowd with mine.
Haile King of Scotland

All. Haile King of Scotland.

Flourish.

  Mal. We shall not spend a large expence of time,
Before we reckon with your seuerall loues,
And make vs euen with you. My Thanes and Kinsmen
Henceforth be Earles, the first that euer Scotland
In such an Honor nam'd: What's more to do,
Which would be planted newly with the time,
As calling home our exil'd Friends abroad,
That fled the Snares of watchfull Tyranny,
Producing forth the cruell Ministers
Of this dead Butcher, and his Fiend-like Queene;
Who (as 'tis thought) by selfe and violent hands,
Tooke off her life. This, and what need full else
That call's vpon vs, by the Grace of Grace,
We will performe in measure, time, and place:

So thankes to all at once, and to each one,
Whom we inuite, to see vs Crown'd at Scone.

Flourish. Exeunt Omnes.

FINIS. THE TRAGEDIE OF MACBETH.

Made in the USA
Middletown, DE
31 October 2020